Book 4 in the
Davina + Quinn
Series

Love's Challenges

Deborah Armstrong

To Tiegan

who asked me to write her a story.

Other books by Deborah Armstrong

Forever Love
Davina + Quinn book 1

Love's Promises
Davina + Quinn book 2

Love's Games
Davina + Quinn book 3

Love's Farewell
Davina + Quinn extra

Boss
Game Changer series

author's note

When I decided to revise and republish my Davina and Quinn series, I knew that *Family Pictures* needed a name change. *Love's Challenges* is the new name. As much as the title, *Family Pictures,* suited the first edition, *Love's Challenges* is perfect for my revised story. Jack and Molly face many challenges—some they face alone, and others they face as a couple.

Love's Challenges is most likely the last book in the series. Readers who have enjoyed being a part of Davina and Quinn's journey will know that our favourite couple is still very much in love. Quinn adores Davina, and she, in return, loves his fussing over her. They make a cameo appearance in this book.

I am writing short stories for those who want to know more about the characters from this series. *Love's Farewell* is the first that came to mind.

Also, on my writing list is adding to the *Game Changer* series. *Bates* is next to make his appearance.

Happy reading,
DEBORAH

prologue

Davina Thomas didn't hear her son standing in the doorway to her office, and yet she felt his presence and the slight ache in her heart that came with knowing that he had awakened to the same nightmare. She kept her gaze on the family pictures covering her office wall while her right hand caressed the silky fur of the sleeping cat purring in her arms.

"It's been a long time," she said. "I thought the dragon had forgotten about us."

"Where would the fun be in that?"

Davina chuckled softly. "You're right. We don't want to get too comfortable in having a normal family life, do we?"

She turned her head to gaze at her son, Jack. He was the image of his father when he was twenty-five years of age. Shaggy dark brown bed head hair framed his perfectly chiselled face and blue eyes. His smile was all hers, though. Not the Hollywood smile Quinn Thomas could force quickly, when necessary, but charming with the promise of mischief.

The dragon was all theirs, too—an inexplicable and unwelcome nightmare that warned them of bad things to come, always to Davina. She bore the scars from the dragon's bite—a gunshot wound, and the reminders of battles won against cancer.

"It was the scariest and silliest dream I think I've ever had. The dragon was standing right here in this spot, and he was forcing you to put his picture on my wall. Right there." Davina nodded her head. "That's your spot."

"My spot?"

"That's reserved for your family picture of you with your ladylove and your children. Next to it is for Stevie with hers, and David's is right below hers."

"Mom, I haven't found my ladylove."

"You will. Some day."

Jack came up behind her and hugged her. His cheek pressed against the side of her head with the silver streak of hair, her dragon's bite. They gazed at the family photographs that had been in Davi's office for as long as Jack could remember. His favourite was of Stevie and him as four-year-olds building a sandcastle on the beach with their father. Quinn told the knight's story with his ladylove and the dragon. Even then, the dragon had been a part of Jack's life.

"What was your dream about, sweetheart?"

"It was scary and silly, too, I guess. I was fighting the dragon. I was fighting him for her. I couldn't see her face, but I could feel her arms wrapped around my waist, holding me tight. We were riding Goliath. All the time, she was whispering in my ear, 'Don't hurt him, he's cute.'"

Davina laughed.

"Crazy. Right?"

"Definitely."

"So, what do you think it means, Mom?"

"That we both had a bit too much to drink at your send-off party last night?"

"Seriously, Mom."

"Maybe, this time, the dragon's not the enemy."

one

Jack Thomas stepped out into the cool morning air and breathed in deeply. There was nothing like fresh air to clear his head after a late night followed by an early morning wake-up call. He shook off the morning chill of April, finished the rest of his black coffee, and threw the empty coffee cup, compliments of the hotel's free breakfast, over-hand into the trash.

"Point," he said aloud, an automatic response caused by too many hours spent on tour with his band.

Everything they did earned points. There were the points based on talent: hitting the garbage pail from the furthest distance, highest score in the various video games they played, and naming a song by its opening chords. There were the points based on juvenile behaviour: loudest belch, loudest and smelliest fart, and the ultimate, silent but deadly fart. Lastly, points were awarded for having the most pairs of panties thrown, or bared breasts flashed at them during a concert. Jack knew that his bandmates awarded points for other activities that he declined to play.

With his guitar case in hand, Jack headed out toward the main street of Ingledale, California. The hotel's desk clerk verified what his GPS had shown him. It would take thirty minutes to walk to the college auditorium. His band's sound check was scheduled for noon, so Jack would have plenty of time to walk and be alone.

Jack liked to walk. Walking was good for thinking. He'd let his feet take him anywhere while he lost himself in thought giving his brain the chance to problem-solve. Sometimes it was a song with a melody or lyrics that weren't quite right. Sometimes, it was working on the right words for a conversation that needed to be had. And sometimes, it was simply the need to be alone.

Walking was also a tactical move to give others time to come around to Jack's way of thinking. He'd learned this strategy from his mother. Jack recalled an instance when his parents were having a heated discussion. He couldn't remember what their argument was about, only that his mom left the house and went for a walk around the farm. His dad sat on the kitchen steps for two hours waiting for her return. When she came back, she said to him, "I'm still right." His father replied, "I know." His mother, Davina Thomas, was always right, and Jack believed that he was, too.

Jack shoved his free hand through his hair and cursed. He didn't want to think about his parents. There were more important things that needed his attention, like his band and their music. They were well into a six-month tour that was sold-out and getting rave reviews. His band, Dragon Slayers, was number one on the charts. Everything should be going great for them, and yet something was wrong, something that was unravelling between the bandmates. Jack was hard pressed to figure out what it was.

Dragon Slayers was the new kid on the block, the rock band that hit the airwaves running and hadn't stopped. Their music had a sound of its own, no one could outplay them, and no one could out sing Jack. His fan base called themselves The Slain, creating fan clubs all over social media.

Was it jealousy? No. Neither Axl, Ben, nor Matt wanted to be the front man for the band. That was Jack's job. He had the looks and the charisma to pull it off. Although Jack worked hard to not take advantage of his last name, he had to admit that being the eldest son of Quinn Thomas, Hollywood's most voted Sexiest Man Alive and multiple Academy Award winner didn't hurt.

Jack regarded the guys in the band as his brothers. They'd been together since the band formed during high school. They always talked things out. Nothing was worth fighting over. No one's ideas were better than the others. But now, Jack couldn't put his finger on it. It didn't matter how this problem started; it was up to Jack to fix it.

XO XO XO

Molly sat at her favourite table in the local coffee shop sipping her double Americano, watching the thunderstorm outside. Sheets of rain pelted down on to the street, soaking pedestrians while causing mini flash floods on the sidewalk. There wasn't an umbrella to be seen.

The weather forecast had called for a two per cent chance of rain. Molly smiled, believing that the odds, no matter how low, would always work against you. Those who had the time to wait out the storm ducked into the coffee shop to take refuge.

Those who made a run to find shelter elsewhere grabbed Molly's attention. She watched them with a storyteller's eye, fantasizing about who they were and their life stories. Molly imagined only wonderful things, and she always made up a life with a happily ever after ending. There was too much bad in the world to let it darken her imagination.

Molly noticed a young man run by—his soaked T-shirt emblazoned with the words, SHIT HAPPENS. She smiled her agreement. *All the time, buddy.*

She kept her gaze focused on the storm outside, mesmerized by the flashes of lightning. Molly thought of her father and the time they drove through a thunderstorm while navigating a winding road through the mountains. There was no shoulder on the road, nowhere to wait out the storm. The wipers worked furiously to clear the windshield without success. Molly knew now that she was too young to appreciate the gravity of the situation, unaware that her father couldn't see where he was on the road, and was terrified that at any moment he could drive the car off the mountain into the valley below.

"Sing to me," her father urged her. "Sing the rain away."

She remembered singing, "You are my Sunshine." It was her father's favourite song; a song they sang for her mother. Molly sang until the rain stopped.

"That's my girl," her father said with a smile. "You've got the magic."

It was one of the last memories Molly had of her father.

"Is this seat taken?" a warm voice caressed her, instantly pulling her out of her daydream and sending shivers down her spine.

Molly looked away from the window with eyes opened wide to find a rain-soaked man holding a steaming cup of coffee in one hand and a battered guitar case in the other. Water dripped from his brown shoulder-length hair onto his black leather jacket.

"May I?" he asked, nodding toward the empty chair at her table.

"Of course! Where are my manners? Sorry." Molly removed her purse from the table and slung the strap over the back of her chair.

"Thanks," he said while leaning his guitar case against the window. He shrugged off his jacket and hung it on the back of his chair. He was soaked through; his black, long-sleeved T-shirt clung to his skin, showing the outline of sculpted muscles. "I didn't know rain was in the forecast," he said, annoyed, as he took his seat. "The sky was so blue, not one cloud, and then that." Jack pointed to the window.

"This area is known for freak thunderstorms this time of the year. It has to do with the mountains. Do you know the phrase, "April showers bring May flowers?"

Jack nodded his head.

"Well, we seem to get lots of thunderstorms in April. The locals don't go outside without their umbrellas." She pointed to her collapsible umbrella on the table.

He smiled at her with amusement. "So, I guess you can tell who the tourists are by the ones who are soaked?"

"Tourists or college students. You'd be surprised at the number of college kids who consider umbrellas unnecessary, or more like a hindrance to looking cool."

Jack laughed in response. "I've never thought of umbrellas in that way."

Molly felt a blush come to her cheek. "Oh, I wasn't talking about you. I mean," she stammered, "I didn't mean to say you're trying to look cool, although you do. Oh geez…"

"Jack Thomas," he said as he held out his hand to Molly. "I'm not a student, only passing through."

"Welcome to Ingledale, Jack Thomas. My name is Molly Maguire." Molly couldn't help but appraise the man who held her hand. His eyes were steel blue set in a perfectly chiseled face softened by an almost boyish mischievous smile. His wet mop of thick, dark hair lay flat against his head. A gold stud brought attention to his right ear lobe. Molly had never seen anything look as sexy on a man. "So, you're a tourist?"

Jack let go of Molly's hand, reluctant to break their connection. She was a delicate beauty with long blonde hair that fell in thick waves past her shoulders. Her eyes were a pale blue or a gray, he couldn't tell from this distance. Her slightly rounded face held the lightest blush, but it was her smile that pulled him in instantly. His heart told him he knew this woman, although he'd never met her before in his life.

Realizing he was staring at her, Jack answered, "Not really. I'm here for a couple nights then moving on." He turned his attention to the deluge outside. "I'm supposed to be somewhere else right now."

"Somewhere important?" Molly asked, disappointed that this gorgeous hunk of man should be anywhere but sitting across from her, sharing this moment.

"Yes, but it's okay. They'll call me when they notice I'm not there."

"They?"

"My band. Jack nodded toward his guitar case. "I'm late for rehearsal."

"You're a musician?"

"I guess you could say that. What about you? What do you do in Ingledale?"

"I own the local bar and grill, Maguire's. It's across the street from the main entrance to the college. If you'd kept walking, you'd have walked right past it."

"If you have a place of your own, what brings you here?" he asked, intrigued.

"Change of scenery." Molly leaned in toward Jack as if confessing a secret. "It's a different crowd in here, quiet. Besides, I like to watch the boulevard and I can't do that from Maguire's. My manager, Jess, is looking after the place while I'm here."

Maguire's was a busy and noisy hangout for the college crowd. The food was good and the draft beer reasonably priced. Although Molly saw a lot from behind the bar at Maguire's, she appreciated the view from the coffee shop best.

"I like a change of scenery, too," Jack agreed. "That's why I got caught in the rain."

"Rain's good luck," Molly said as though it were an undeniable truth.

"You think so?"

"Yes, I do." Molly drank from her coffee cup before continuing. "Rain washes away the old and lets new things begin afresh. Have you ever watched the sun come out after a thunderstorm and marvelled at how everything is different? The air is fresher and cleaner, and even the birds sing a different tune."

"Don't forget the beautiful rainbows that follow."

"And the rainbows," Molly agreed.

Jack pointed to his empty coffee cup. "Would you like another? My treat."

Molly answered with a smile. "Please. Double Americano. No sugar."

"You like your coffee strong."

"It's the only way to drink it."

Molly watched as Jack took their empty cups to the counter and ordered two Americanos. He was tall, about six foot three inches. His wet shirt accentuated his broad shoulders and lean body. Faded designer jeans showed off his assets—long muscled legs attached to a gorgeous ass. He was perfection on two legs. Molly's shoulders slumped as she realized the reason behind his perfection—he was gay. Her gaydar was never wrong. That explained why she didn't catch him checking out her chest; his focus was only on her face. Molly sighed, accepting that her fantasy man would be only that—a coffee break fantasy.

As he placed his coffee order, Jack felt the stares of the female patrons. He was used to it. He'd learned from his dad that it came with the territory. *They'll stare at you and undress you with their eyes, Jack. Let them. If you have one woman who wants you for who you are inside, the rest won't matter.*

Jack returned to the table with their Americanos. "There's cream in both. I know you didn't ask for cream, but the server insisted."

Molly looked over at the counter and gave a small wave to the server. "Alice has been serving me my morning coffee for a very long time. Thank you."

"You're welcome." Jack caught himself staring at her. She wore a bit of make-up, just enough to highlight her eyes and add colour to her full and inviting lips.

"Are you in a real band?"

"Like a bar band?"

"Yes. Like a bar band. Sometimes I hire a band for weekends. Is your band any good?"

"You wouldn't want us," Jack said, looking down at his coffee.

"That bad?"

"No. We're good. We're not playing in bars right now."

"Struggling to get heard?"

"Just struggling."

Jack should have told her who he was, but he liked this moment of anonymity. It was a rarity and he hated to ruin it.

"It will work out for you," Molly said.

"How do you know that?"

"The rain has stopped and there's a double rainbow crossing the sky. That has to bring you good luck."

"Have you always been so optimistic?" Jack resisted the urge to take her hand, sure that he'd feel her positive energy.

She shook her head no and chuckled. "I wish. Once I realized that there was no use in seeing the bad in everything, I figured that if I tried to see only the good, then maybe the good would stay with me. Believe me, some days it's a struggle, but there's always a lot more good than bad.

"My mom is like that," Jack said thoughtfully. "Despite some of the crap she's had to go through, she's still the eternal optimist."

"What about your dad?"

"My mom is his world. As long as she's happy, he's happy."

"Mmm, sounds romantic. You must come from a happy family."

Jack smiled. "You have no idea. What about you?"

"My dad died when I was eight. Mom remarried and I don't get along well with her husband."

"I'm sorry about your dad. I can't imagine not having mine around."

"Oh, he's around me every day," Molly said cheerfully. "When you drop by my bar, you'll see his pictures everywhere. I'll introduce you to him." Molly couldn't believe the words as they left her mouth. Her cheeks blushed a brilliant red, and her eyes opened wide. She had never been so brazen with a man without the security of her oak bar standing between them while she held a baseball bat. "I'm sorry," she stammered. "You must think I'm crazy."

"Not at all. You're not the only one who surrounds yourself with family pictures. Maybe I can show you mine sometime." Jack's cellphone buzzed. He looked at the screen and typed a message. "I have to go. I've been missed."

Molly reached into her bag and pulled out her business card and handed it to Jack. "Drop by Maguire's and have a drink on the house. If you've got your guitar, maybe you can play for us."

"I'd like that." Jack read the card before putting it in his wallet. He didn't want to leave and break their connection. "There's a concert tonight. Dragon Slayers is playing. Have you heard of them?"

"They're a new band, aren't they? Our DJ has been playing one of their songs—something about being lonely."

"It's called, 'I'm Lonely.' If I leave a ticket for you at the gate, will you come? I'll be working so I can't sit with you, but afterwards we can go out for drinks or a late dinner."

Molly couldn't resist his eyes. They were pleading with her to say yes. What did it matter if Jack was gay? She liked him, and it had been a long time since she'd gone out with a man, gay or straight.

"Yes. I'd love to go. Thank you."

"Great. I'll have a pass waiting for you at the gate." Jack stood and pulled on his damp leather jacket. He reached for his guitar case and faced Molly. "I'll see you later, Molly."

"Bye, Jack. Later."

Molly watched Jack leave the cafe and then make his way along the boulevard heading toward the college campus. He walked tall, holding his head high with his shoulders pushed back. His ass—Molly gave her head a shake and sighed.

two

Her song came to him as easily as breathing. Its melody, though simple, was haunting. Jack couldn't get it out of his head as he hummed the new tune while making his way to the auditorium. It was in four-four time, five simple verses divided by a poignant chorus.

He stopped when he realized he'd arrived at Maguire's. From the outside, Maguire's seemed inviting. A patio with tables and bright red umbrellas with Maguire's emblazoned on the sides ready for warmer weather. Over the entranceway hung a wood carved sign with Maguire's. A neon sign flashed OPEN from inside the windows. Resisting the temptation to look inside, Jack decided to wait for Molly to give him the tour.

Molly was right. The entrance to the college campus was across the street. Jack pushed the pedestrian button for the crosswalk before taking his cellphone out of his jacket pocket to make a call.

"Hello," a male voice answered with a low mumble.

"Dad, are you okay?"

"You caught me," his father chuckled heartily. "I'm in bed with the most beautiful woman in the world."

Jack smiled. "How is Mom?"

"She's resting. She had her last round of radiation this morning. Handled it like a champ."

"Any news from her doctor?"

"No. We meet with him next week once all the test results are in. We're hopeful that the cancer's gone. What's up?" His father didn't waste time getting to the point.

"I found her, Dad."

"Good for you. Have you professed your love for her, or are you going to take your time?"

Jack heard his mother's voice in the background, asking for the phone.

"Take your time, sweetheart. Professing your love on the first day isn't the wisest decision."

"You and Dad did that."

"Your father did that, Jackie. It took me longer to agree. I fought him on it for the longest time."

"Three days," his father said loud enough for Jack to hear. "I knew from the moment I saw her she was the one. Love at first sight, Jack."

Jack waited for a moment. He knew his parents were kissing. Whenever one of them mentioned love at first sight, they had to kiss, as though they were renewing their love.

"Take your time," Davina Thomas said. "There's no rush."

"I want what you and Dad have. I'm ready."

His mother sighed. "What is it with you Thomas men? You decide you're ready to settle down, and instantly you find the woman of your dreams. Can't you meet a nice girl and date for awhile?"

Jack laughed. "It's not the Thomas way, Mom."

"How are you? Are you enjoying the tour? Is Axl behaving? I worry about him."

"Axl's fine, Mom. And yes, the tour's going great so far." There was no point in telling his mother his concerns about the band. Not until he found out for himself.

"When are you coming home? I miss you."

He could hear the fatigue in her voice. Jack closed his eyes and forced the tears away. *She's going to be fine. Dad said so.*

"Soon, I promise."

"It's me," his father said. "Come home soon, Jack, and bring your girlfriend. I've got to look after this beauty in my bed. We love you."

"I will. Talk to you later." Jack ended the call and pocketed his phone.

Quinn Thomas was head over heels in love with his wife, and Davina loved him with all her heart. They never held back in showing their love. Jack was raised in a loving family with parents who believed in and lived the happily ever after love story. Was he foolish to want the same?

XO XO XO

"Thanks for showing up," Axl shouted when he noticed Jack making his way to the stage from the front doors. "I guess being on time doesn't apply to some of us."

Jack stiffened at the snide remark, caught off guard by the coldness in the bass player's tone. He yelled back, "I didn't expect to get caught in the rain, and I knew you'd start without me. What's the problem?"

"If you expect all of us to be on time, then damn it, you sure as hell should be on time. You couldn't take the bus with us? You had to walk? How hard can it be to get from the hotel to this place? I bet your mother could make it here on time."

"Hey, leave my mother out of this."

Jack ran up the front stairs to the stage and stopped two feet from the burly bass player. He fixed his gaze on Axl's rugged face. They were the same height, although Axl was about twenty pounds heavier. Jack had the advantage of lean muscle and fighting ability. Years of working out with his father made sure that Jack could look after himself if needed.

"I apologize for being late. If you have something to get off your chest, man, say it now."

"I've got nothing to say to you. We've already wasted enough time." Axl turned his head and spat on the floor.

"Okay, then. I want to play something for you."

Jack turned and walked over to his assortment of guitars lined up in front of his microphone. He placed his guitar case on the floor and opened it, taking out his favourite acoustic guitar, a Martin D-28.

"What have you got?" Axl asked, watching Jack handle his guitar with loving care.

"I came up with this while I was walking here," Jack said while he tuned his guitar. He strummed a few chords tentatively before a melodic tune flowed from his fingers. Turning to his bandmates, he waited for their reaction.

Axl listened, nodding his head for the first verse before adding a bass line to the song. Their drummer, Ben, followed with percussion, and Matt joined with rhythm guitar. Fifteen minutes later, the band had created a new song. The four men stopped and stared at each other with boyish grins.

"Just like old times," Axl said, nodding his head. "That's a keeper, Jack. What's it called?"

"Molly's Rain."

"You named it after a girl? It figures," Ben teased.

"Where'd you meet this one?" Matt asked.

"At a coffee shop. I invited her to tonight's concert. Think we can fit this in?"

"Sure. It will feel good to play something we all like," Axl answered.

"Finally," Matt said.

"I hope she likes it," Ben said. "If not, we can always change the name."

"Me, too," Jack said while he placed his acoustic guitar with the others. He selected his Gibson electric guitar and returned to centre stage.

"Where did you disappear to last night?" Ben called out to him. "There was this girl that wouldn't stop asking about you. Even while she was blowing me, she kept saying your name. It was fucking unreal."

"Don't you lose points if the girl calls out some other dude's name while your dick is in her mouth?" Axl asked while winking at Jack.

"Double if it's Jack's," Matt added.

"Keep me out of this," Jack warned them as he plugged in his guitar. "It's your side game, boys. Your points."

"Who cares about points? We won't need them for much longer." The somber tone of Ben's voice killed whatever levity the band was feeling.

"What the hell are you talking about?" Jack asked.

"You still haven't told us where you went after the concert, man. No one could find you. What's the big secret?" Axl asked.

"There's no secret," Jack answered, feeling the hairs on the back of his neck bristle. "I went to the bus. That's all."

"Sure, it is," Ben said.

"Are you calling me a liar?"

"Okay, enough already," Axl shouted. "We're here to play. If Jack has anything to tell us, he will. Won't you, Jack?"

Axl didn't wait for Jack to answer. "Ben, count us in."

Jack knew that look on Axl's face—his mouth pulled tight, and eyes narrowed to dark slits told Jack that he wasn't off the hook. Axl was angry, reinforcing Jack's feeling that something was wrong with the band. Axl was right. Now was not the time to talk about the band. They were running late. Their music came first. Everything and everyone else came second.

three

Molly hadn't been out on a date in months. It wasn't that she hadn't had the opportunity. There were college students who had asked her out, but she had grown out of that stage in her life. She needed someone who could settle her. She wasn't looking for the wedding band and a house full of kids. Molly wasn't ready for that. It was more like needing a man who could love her, and she could love in return—a man that got her and who didn't make her want to kick him to the curb after a month or two of dating.

She took one last look at herself in her bedroom mirror. It may have been ages since she last attended a rock concert, but Molly knew how to dress for it. She pulled her thick blonde hair into a messy ponytail. Large gold hoop earrings made the perfect accessory to her form-fitting glitter T-shirt tucked into a black leather mini skirt. A black belt cinched in at her trim waist, a short black leather jacket and high-heeled black leather boots finished the look. Molly grabbed her clutch bag before heading off to the concert.

As promised, a ticket waited for her at the auditorium's ticket booth. Molly was surprised to find that her seat was front row centre. It was a single seat. Jack wouldn't be sitting with her. Disappointed that she'd be enjoying the concert without Jack's company, Molly looked forward to seeing Jack afterwards. He had promised her drinks or a late dinner. Still, hopeful that she might get a glimpse of the handsome stranger, Molly sat on the edge of her seat and looked for him. He hadn't said what his job was, and she hadn't thought to ask. She assumed that he was a roadie the way his wet shirt clung to his chest and showed off the defined muscles underneath. Moving heavy equipment would be his workout.

Molly sipped her beer. Her attention now focused on the people sitting near her. They were her age, mid-twenties or younger. She watched the women check their reflections in their compacts, making sure they looked perfect, and then tug at their tops in a last-minute attempt to expose as much cleavage as possible.

"Looking good," Molly said to the girls sitting to her right. "You only live once, right?"

"Hell, yes, girl!" one of the girls shouted out while the rest pumped their fists in the air.

Molly sat back in her seat. Oh, to be young and foolish. She had no desire to get noticed by anyone in the band. She had dated a musician once. More like a wannabe musician. She hired him to play in her bar a few times. His music was average, and his bedroom skills were below that.

The lights dimmed, and the audience cheered.

"All the way from Toronto, Canada, please welcome Dragon Slayers!" the announcer's voice boomed over the sound system.

Molly didn't know the band except for the one song she had heard in her bar. She wished now that she had paid attention to the posters lining the auditorium's lobby. Instead, she scanned the crowd for a glimpse of Jack.

She applauded and cheered with the rest of the audience as the members of the band took their places on the darkened stage. The lead singer and guitarist stopped at centre stage and turned his back to the audience. Molly's gaze went at once to the black leather pants covering long legs and an irresistible ass. He wore black leather from head to toe. Dark shaggy hair hung down to the collar of his jacket.

"Nice," she said, nodding, as she continued to admire the rest of the singer's body.

The drummer counted out the beat before the band joined in with an explosive intro that led into the only song familiar to Molly. She screamed with the others, urging the lead singer to turn around to face them. At last, the lead singer of Dragon Slayers turned around and looked directly at Molly.

Molly put her hand to her mouth when she recognized Jack. She never thought he'd be in the band. Why would she? He told her his name, but not much else. *Idiot.*

Molly sighed. Jack sang, his rich tenor voice, silky smooth and pitch perfect reached out to her and caressed her. She sat mesmerized, listening to every word he sang. She didn't follow those who rushed to the stage, screaming and waving at Jack. She had the perfect view of Jack, and she knew that he was watching her with his brilliant blue eyes.

If she'd had a dream like this, tonight would be that dream come true. Having a man sing to her making her feel like she was the only woman in the world thrilled her. She sat still and listened to Jack Thomas, lead singer of the Dragon Slayers, sing every song to her. When she thought the night couldn't get any better, it did.

"And now I'd like to sing something the band and I wrote today. It's called 'Molly's Rain.' I hope you like it."

The audience went quiet as Jack picked up his acoustic guitar and sat on a stool. The stage went dark except for a single light shining down on him. Again, Jack focused his gaze on Molly.

"She sat by the window staring at the rain,
She said rain brings good luck, you know,
It washes away the bad, washes away the pain."

Molly sat entranced by his voice. She let the tears stream down her face, not bothering to wipe them away. They'd just met, sharing a table and drinking Americanos. He didn't have to write her a song. He didn't have to sing about falling in love with her. Could he have fallen in love with her? Molly's eyes opened wide. Did that mean Jack Thomas was straight?

While the audience cheered and applauded 'Molly's Rain,' Molly remained motionless in her seat, still reeling from Jack's proclamation of love. *Get real, Molly. It's a love song. He used your name. That's all. Love at first sight does not happen. Are you in love with Jack? No. Then it's not love at first sight. It's a love song. Take a breath. Smile. Listen to the music.*

Molly did just that. She took in a breath, let it out, smiled at Jack and then sat back in her seat ready to listen to Jack sing more songs.

The lights brightened and Jack got up from his stool. He traded guitars with a stagehand. The drummer beat out a thumping rhythm and the bassist joined in, followed by the other guitarist.

Jack took off his leather jacket and tossed it to Molly. She caught it and clutched it to her chest. She glared at anyone who dared to touch it.

"It's getting hot in here," Jack shouted out to the audience as he winked at Molly. "I hope you don't mind if I take my shirt off."

The audience cheered. The girls sitting beside Molly gave out a deafening shriek. Their arms outstretched to the stage, their hands waving wildly hoping to catch his shirt as he threw it into the crowd.

Molly stared at Jack in disbelief. "No," she said, terrified at the sight of his chest. "Please, no." She squeezed her eyes shut and recited her mantra, "They're only tattoos. They will not hurt me. It was a man who killed my father, not tattoos. There is nothing to fear. Pictures can't hurt me. I am safe." She repeated her mantra blocking out Jack and the music.

When the song ended, Molly prayed that Jack would put on a shirt. She waited to hear his voice before she dared open her eyes. He remained shirtless, his sweat covered torso glistening under the lights, making the tattoos look alive. Frightening. One look at Jack and panic took over. She was terrified of tattoos, not of the people who had them. It was what tattoos represented to her—monsters, evil, and death. Every memory of her father's vicious murder slammed into her.

Molly couldn't stay and look at Jack one minute longer. She had to leave. There was no thought of Jack who watched her in bewilderment. She had to escape the terror that gripped her insides. Molly got to her feet and pushed her way through the crowd while hugging Jack's jacket to her chest. She found her way to an exit and ran out of the auditorium, not stopping until she made it to the safety of Maguire's.

Molly yanked open the doors to Maguire's and stood in the doorway and caught her breath. She inhaled the smells she'd known all of her life—stale beer, fried food, and sweat. She was home. Safe. She made her way behind the bar and pulled out a lowball glass, filling it to the brim with Jack Daniels whiskey. Molly took two swallows of the amber liquor before she acknowledged the woman watching her.

"You look like you've seen a ghost," Jess, her bartender and best friend, said, watching Molly take another drink from her glass. "I thought you were out on a date."

Molly nodded her head in agreement while topping up her glass.

"Did he try to rape you? Why do you have his coat?" Jess whispered.

Jess nodded to the other bartender to take over as she grabbed a glass for herself and the bottle of Jack Daniels before pushing Molly toward the office. Jess stepped in front of Molly to unlock the door and stepped aside for Molly to enter ahead of her.

Molly sat heavily on the old leather couch, spilling her drink while still clutching Jack's leather jacket. She ignored the wet spot on her skirt, focusing on gulping down the rest of her whiskey.

"What happened?" Jess demanded, while refilling both of their glasses.

Jess sat beside Molly and nudged her with her elbow.

"He's Jack Thomas of the Dragon Slayers. He invited me to his concert."

Jess gasped. "You didn't know who he was?"

"No! He just said he was in a band, and he was working tonight at the auditorium. I thought that he was a roadie or something like that. He offered to get me a ticket and then said we could meet for drinks or dinner later. He never said he was in the band."

"He's covered in tattoos! What were you thinking?"

"I didn't know about his tattoos! He had all of his clothes on when I met him. Geez, Jess." Molly took a sip from her glass.

"You didn't tell him about—"

"Do I look like an idiot, Jess? I meet a guy in a coffee shop and say to him, By the way, you don't have any tattoos do you, because if you do, I can't date you. Why? Oh, I'll just be scared shitless, that's all. That would go over well." Molly finished her glass and motioned for a refill, her hand shaking. "Besides, I thought he was gay."

Jess choked on her drink. "Gay? Are you crazy? That man's hundred percent straight. It's his sister who's gay."

"Fill it." Molly moved her glass closer to the bottle.

"I think you've had enough."

"I can still see them, Jess. Every one of those monsters. I haven't had enough."

"I'm sorry," Jess said softly as she poured more Jack Daniels into Molly's glass.

"Me, too. I think he likes me, or at least he did until I ran out of his concert. He wrote me a love song."

"No kidding."

"It's called 'Molly's Rain.' It's beautiful." Molly wiped away a tear. "Damn it. He won't be back. Not after what happened."

"Maybe he didn't see you leave. Maybe—"

"I was front row centre. His eyes were on me the whole time. He saw me run out of there. I'm sure of it."

"If he didn't know about your—"

"It doesn't matter. Once tattooed guys know how messed up I am, they don't stick around for long. You know that. Who would stay with a girl he couldn't get naked with?"

"He could get naked. You'd just have to wear a blindfold."

"Oh, that would go over well," Molly drawled. The liquor finally affecting her.

Jess squeezed Molly's hand. "Do you want me to stay with you?"

"No. I'm okay, thanks. We have a full house tonight. You should be behind the bar." Molly gave Jess a weak smile. "I'll stay here for a bit and watch some television. Call me if you need me."

Jess stood and gazed down at her friend. "I could kill that son of a bitch for what he did to you."

"He's already dead, Jess. There's nothing you can do except help keep his ghost away."

"I'll see you at closing," Jess said as she walked to the office door. "Take it easy," she added before closing the door behind her.

Molly reached for the remote and turned on the television. She selected her favourite Friday night sitcom and then stretched out on the couch still holding on to Jack's leather jacket.

four

Jack didn't stay for the after-concert party. He was fuming mad. How dare she walk out on him! Molly wouldn't look at him. She just got up and ran out. Jack peeled off his leather pants and threw them on the floor, then yanked on his faded jeans and a muscle man shirt of Ben's that he found hanging over a chair. Jack pulled on his boots and exited the auditorium, not caring what he looked like as he headed for Maguire's.

Jess recognized him at once. Most of the crowd in the bar recognized him, as well, but Jack didn't seem to notice. She nodded to him as he approached the bar.

"You came."

"So, she's here?" he asked roughly.

"She's in her office. Can I get you a drink?"

"I have to talk to Molly first."

"First, you need to put a shirt on. Muscle man shirts aren't allowed in here." Jess pointed to the large sign behind the bar.

"She has my jacket."

"I know, but you still have to have a shirt on before you can see her."

"I don't have one," Jack bit out, pissed off with the delay.

"It just so happens that we sell them." Jess reached behind her and handed him an extra-large long-sleeved shirt, black with the Maguire's logo on the chest. "This should fit. It's twenty bucks."

"I have to pay for it?" Jack asked, incredulous.

"If you want to talk to Molly, you have to buy it, and you have to wear it. It could be the best twenty bucks you've ever spent." She smiled sweetly at him.

Jack pulled out his wallet and fished out a twenty-dollar bill and a ten. "For the shirt and my drink," he said while handing her the money.

"The drink's on the house, but I'll donate the tenner. Thanks." Jess stuffed the ten-dollar bill into a red jar behind the bar.

Jess poured a double of Jack Daniels and watched him put on the shirt. She sighed as the material stretched across his broad chest. It was a shame to cover up that chest, although necessary for Molly's sake.

Jess handed Jack his drink.

"I'd prefer beer," he snapped.

"And I'd prefer to be a 36D," Jess answered back. "But we don't always get what we want." She nodded toward the office door. "She's in there. Be nice and listen to what she has to say. Please, listen."

XO XO XO

Molly heard a light rap at her door. Thinking it was Jess, she called out, "Come in!"

The door opened, and Jack entered and closed the door behind him. Molly looked over at him and scrambled to sit up on the couch.

"Hi," she said, quickly wiping away her tears with the back of her hand. "Thank you for my song. It's beautiful."

"You're welcome," Jack murmured, chastened by Molly's appearance. He intended to have it out with her and demand why she ran out on him. But the woman he saw before him looked like she'd already suffered enough, evidenced by the smeared makeup, bloodshot eyes, and piles of used tissues on the floor.

"Would you like a drink?" Molly motioned to the half-empty bottle of Jack Daniels.

Jack raised his glass. "I've already got one. You drink this stuff?" he asked with mock horror. He hadn't acquired a taste for hard liquor. Beer was more his style.

"On nights like these, it's the only thing that helps."

"What happened?" Jack asked. "Did someone do something to you? I saw you leave. Running like you were scared to death."

Molly nodded her head in agreement. "You're right. I was scared to death, but no one did anything to me, not tonight, anyway."

"What? You're not making any sense."

She stood up and offered her hand to him. "Let me introduce you to my dad."

"Now?"

"Yes, now."

Jack took her hand. Molly led him behind her desk to the wall covered with framed photographs. She pointed to the first one and then started her story.

"This is me when I was eight years old, my dad, Angus, and my mom, Nancy. The picture was taken here at the bar. Dad was celebrating the fifth anniversary of Maguire's opening. He was happy, and so was I because it was the first time I could remember being allowed to stay in the bar when they were serving alcohol."

"Your hair was quite blonde," Jack remarked.

"I'm a natural blonde, only smarter," Molly said with pride. She was used to the blonde jokes.

"I didn't mean—"

"It's okay," Molly interrupted him. She pointed to more pictures on the wall. They were all family pictures taken at the bar. "One day, Mom had to go out shopping. I was at home because my school had closed for repairs. Something about water damage from too much rainfall. I didn't want to go with Mom, so Dad let me stay with him.

Back then, Maguire's wasn't a hangout for the college kids. Since it was a weekday, business would be slow. The regular customers didn't start to come in until after work, so my dad knew that I wouldn't be in the way. I remember watching him polish the glasses and make sure everything was sparkling behind the bar. He was so proud of this place. He loved to show it off. Dad made me a cherry cola and then I sat in my favourite booth and spent the rest of the morning playing with my dolls and colouring."

Jack's gaze focused on a framed newspaper clipping. The heading read, "*Local bar owner butchered in front of daughter.*" He ran his free hand through his hair and cursed.

Molly started to explain with a steady voice, "This man came in. He demanded cash from my dad. Dad said he could take what he had, but it wasn't much. It was too early in the day." Molly pointed to the murderer's mugshot. "He didn't believe my dad. He jumped over the bar and stabbed him. I sat there and didn't say a word. I was so afraid that he'd get me, too."

"You were very lucky."

"He opened the cash register and took out the cash. There was blood everywhere—on his shirt and his hands. I remember watching him taking off his shirt and wiping my dad's blood off his hands with it. That's when I saw all of his tattoos. They covered him from his face right down to the waist. Even his arms were a mass of colour."

"Geez."

"Then he left, and I ran to my dad. He was dead. I remember phoning the police and telling them to come—that the coloured man had killed him." Molly closed her eyes as she remembered that day. "It was a nightmare. I was a child. I had never seen tattoos before; I just thought of them as colours. That's why I called him a coloured man. It had taken the longest time before the police understood what I meant. They were about to round up every black man in the area."

"They caught him." Jack pointed to the killer's picture in the newspaper article.

"It's hard to hide something like that, wouldn't you say?" Molly snorted in disgust. "He killed my dad for a hundred bucks. That's all that was in the till, Jack, one hundred dollars. My dad's life was worth more than that."

Molly moved along the wall. There were various pictures taken through the years of Molly with her mother.

"Mom kept the bar running. We had nowhere else to go, and the bar was all my mom knew how to run. When I was old enough, I started working here. I wanted to keep this place. It's the only memory I have of my dad. When Mom remarried, her husband wanted to move away; it was the perfect time for me to take over the bar."

"So, when you saw my tattoos—"

"I was scared shitless."

"You thought I was a monster?"

"Not you, but I saw monsters."

"Did you think I would hurt you? Do you think I'll hurt you now?"

"I'm not afraid of you. I'm terrified of tattoos. I see them and all I see are monsters. The images of my father's murder flashing through my mind are so vivid and horrifying that I call them the ghosts."

"I don't understand," he shook his head.

"As long as you wear a shirt, as long as I don't see a trace of colour on you, I can be with you. See? I'm not afraid of you. You can touch me. I can touch you." She reached out and caressed his cheek. "But I can never look at your tattoos."

"That's why I had to buy this shirt before your bartender would let me see you," Jack said, now understanding.

"No one is served if there is any trace of a full torso tattoo. I can handle a bit of ink on the arms if the tattoos are spaced apart, but not full arm sleeves." She shuddered. "They're a real trigger for me." A smile broke across her face. "We sell a lot of shirts that way."

"Good business move," Jack said with a chuckle.

"It all goes to a charity for victims of violence."

"I'm sorry. If I'd known—"

"Don't," Molly interrupted. "There was no way it would have ever come up in our conversation this morning."

"When does it come up in a conversation?"

"It would have come up tonight, remember? I told you I'd introduce you to my dad. These pictures are the only way I can talk about my fear of tattoos."

"Speaking of tonight," Jack said cautiously. "I promised to take you out for drinks and dinner. I have the drink, and I could eat. How's Maguire's food?"

Molly smiled warmly at him. "Let's go. Dinner is on me." She took him by the hand and led him back to the bar where she found a booth away from the noise of the after-concert crowd.

"Stay here," she told Jack before she left for the kitchen.

"How's it going?" Jess asked her as she passed by the bar.

"We're talking," Molly answered. "Take him a beer, will you please? He doesn't drink hard liquor." She didn't wait for a reply as she pushed open the door into the kitchen. "One burger with everything, a spinach salad with salmon, and a plate of nachos with extra cheese, please," she called out. "Bring it to booth thirteen. Thanks, guys."

Molly returned to the bar and poured herself a draft beer before she rejoined Jack. When she made it back to their booth she found Jack texting on his cell phone, smiling as he did so.

"Anything I should know?" she asked.

"It's my dad. I told him you ran out on me. He told me the ones who are worth it always do."

Molly shook her head. "I didn't run out on you exactly."

"Yes, you did, but that's okay. We'll try again tomorrow." Jack pocketed his cell phone as he gazed at Molly. "You're coming to the concert tomorrow."

"No," she argued. "I can't."

Jack took her hand. "I promise that I will not shed one item of clothing in front of you. I will keep myself covered." His gaze searched her face for understanding. "Tonight, was only a dress rehearsal, so to speak. Tomorrow I'll get it right."

"You don't have to. Your fans expect to see you and your—" Molly pointed at his chest.

"Did you see them?"

"Not really. Just the colours. That's all it takes."

"So, you have absolutely no idea what my tattoos look like, do you?"

"No. And I don't want to know." Molly stared back at him in defiance.

"Aren't you in the least bit curious?"

She blew out in frustration. "I told you that you're fine as long as you stay covered. If you keep pushing this, you might as well leave now."

Jack sat back, keeping his eyes locked on hers. "I saw yours."

"I don't have tattoos."

"You have those family photos in your office. You even have them out here in the bar. Look around you, Molly. You've got your family on every wall in this place."

"They're pictures, Jack. They're pictures of my family, and they mean something to me."

"So are mine. Every drop of ink means something to me. Every picture reminds me of my family. Every tattoo pays tribute to someone I love."

"Please, Jack."

"I won't say another word but think about it. I can stay covered up, but it doesn't hide the fact that I have the right to show off my family as much as you do yours."

Jess arrived with their platter of nachos. She could see the tension between them. "Everything all right here?" she asked Molly as she placed the platter on the table.

"We're fine," Molly answered. "We're talking about family."

"I bet you are," Jess said under her breath before she walked away.

Jack popped a nacho into his mouth. He watched Molly picking at the cheese on hers. He wondered if she knew how beautiful she was with her hair pulled back loosely from her face, the rosy glow on her cheeks and the slight smudge of mascara under her eyes. That mouth—what he wouldn't do to have a taste of those luscious lips. Jack could feel himself harden. *Not a chance*, he thought to himself, but he knew that brain thought differently. Jack drained his beer.

"Another one?" Molly asked.

"Sure. Thanks."

Molly left to get another beer from the bar. Jack couldn't resist the urge to watch her as she walked. Damn she was a beauty. Jack turned back and focused on the plate of nachos. Chasing after a woman who wouldn't let him near her was going to be a difficult challenge, but not impossible.

"He watched your ass as you walked over here," Jess said, glowering at Jack as Molly poured them both another beer.

"Good," Molly said happily. "I wanted him to."

"Why in heaven's name would you do that? You don't want him near you. Do you?" Jess stopped in front of Molly, refusing to let her pass without answering.

"I don't know," Molly answered, turning her attention to Jack. "I like him, Jess. He's gorgeous, and he likes me. He hasn't run for the hills yet either."

"Maybe he will once he gets in your pants. Have you thought of that, Molly? What if you're just a challenge to him, another notch in the rock star's belt?"

"What if he's just another notch in my belt? Can't I do the same?"

Jess joined Molly in looking at Jack. "That will not be a notch in your belt, missy. That will leave a mark on you that you'll never forget."

"Like a tattoo?"

"You're terrified of tattoos!"

"I know, but what if—" Molly shook her head. "I'm talking shit, Jess. It's the liquor getting to me. That's all. Forget I said anything." Molly kissed Jess's cheek then headed back to Jack with two glasses of beer.

Their dinner order was on the table waiting for them. Jack had started eating his burger.

"Sorry," he apologized. "I couldn't wait. Great burger. My dad would love it here."

"Your dad's into burgers?"

"Big time. He knows every great burger joint in the world. I guess I do, too. He's taken me to most of them."

"Your father is Quinn Thomas," Molly said as she realized the resemblance.

"Yes," Jack smiled up at her, his eyes sparkling. "Are you a fan of his?"

"Of course," Molly gushed. "What's it like to have him for a father?"

"He's real if you know what I mean. He always puts family first. He's crazy about my mom. I don't know what he'd do if anything happened to her." Jack stared at his plate and went quiet.

"Jack?" Molly reached out to touch his arm.

"I can't talk about it. There's stuff going on with my family right now. Sorry."

"Don't apologize. It's okay."

Jack looked at Molly. "Enough talking. This burger is begging to get eaten."

Molly pushed her plate away and sat back and watched Jack devour his burger. She sipped her beer, wondering what he would be like in bed. Would he devour her as lustfully as he did the burger? She could feel a tingle course through her body. How long had it been since she last had a lover? She shuddered to think of how long it had been.

Jack finished his burger and washed it down with a long drink of beer. He pushed the empty plate away and smiled his adorable mischievous grin at Molly.

"You enjoyed that."

"Yes, I did. Thank you."

"You're welcome. It's the least I could do after leaving you the way I did."

"You're right. It is the least you could do."

Jack stood up from the table and offered his hand to her. "Let's dance."

Recorded dance music played in the background. Molly hadn't danced in ages. She gave him her hand. Jack's hand pressed lightly against the small of her back as he guided her to the crowded dance floor. In one smooth move, he turned Molly around, pulled her body into his and started dancing. Molly breathed in his scent. He smelled of beer and sweat. She pulled away from him slightly.

"Sorry, for the smell. I didn't shower after the show. I came right here."

"It's okay. I like the smell of beer."

Jack gazed down at her with a doubtful look. "Seeing the good in the bad, are you?"

Molly laughed. "I'll dance with you no matter how bad you smell. How's that?"

"Perfect," Jack answered, laughing as he pulled her in close again and moved with her across the dance floor.

They danced until the last call. Jack didn't want to let go of Molly, and Molly wanted desperately to be held by Jack if only this one time.

Molly led Jack to her office and closed the door behind them. Jack headed for the leather couch and took a seat. He watched Molly dim the lights, and smiled, enjoying the sexy sway of her hips as she made her way toward him.

"I've had a wonderful time tonight," her voice was soft and lusty.

"So have I."

She stopped at his feet, gazing down at him. "I have rules that have to be followed, especially because of your condition."

Jack grimaced. "It's not a condition, Molly. I'm not sick."

Molly held up her hand to silence him. "Jack, this is a big risk for me. Please understand that."

Jack nodded. "I do understand. Just tell me what you want."

"Kissing only. No removal of clothes, especially yours."

"I can do that," Jack said, smiling.

"And no touching."

"No touching?" Jack's eyebrow arched.

"Let's kiss first. That is if you want to. Do you want to kiss me, Jack?" She licked her upper lip and then the lower lip slowly, seductively.

"Ah, hell, Molly," Jack groaned as he reached for her and pulled her onto his lap.

Her lips were as soft and sweet as he had imagined. His kiss was slow and gentle. Jack wanted to savour every moment of Molly's taste. Her tongue found his, coaxing him to give more and he did. It was a hot kiss. It was wild. It was wonderful.

Molly's hands instantly went to his hair. She pulled at it, twining it through her long, slender fingers. Jack moaned at the slight pain and the pleasure that followed. His hands pressed against her back, keeping her tight against him. He fought the urge to pull up the back of her shirt and feel her soft skin. He wouldn't risk ruining a kiss like this.

Needing more, Molly moved to straddle Jack. She rubbed against him, feeling his hard erection beneath his jeans. Despite her rule for no touching, her body wanted him. Her sensitive nipples pressed against her tank top, aching for his touch and his mouth. She didn't care. She felt the dampness between her legs increasing. All she had to do was give him the word, and she knew he'd be inside her.

Jack's arousal strained against his zipper. If Molly was testing him, he was about to fail miserably. Her constant grinding against his crotch was undoing him. Kissing her like this was only going to lead to one thing and he couldn't risk it.

Jack broke away from their kiss. "No," he moaned. "We can't do this." He gripped her arms and pushed her away.

Her lips were red and swollen. Her eyelids were heavy with the arousal that flowed through her veins. "We can, Jack," Molly said, reaching for him, needing more of him.

Jack pulled away again. "You said only kissing."

"I want more."

"We can't!"

"We can. Just don't take off your shirt. We'll be fine." Molly's hands dropped to his crotch; her fingers worked at his zipper. It didn't take much effort to release his cock from his jeans.

"Molly," Jack pleaded. "Please."

"I want you, Jack. Let me do this."

"No. Molly. Stop."

Molly stopped. She looked at Jack, staring deep into his eyes. "Oh my god, you're gay, aren't you? I knew it!"

"No, I'm not gay," Jack sputtered.

"Are you clean?"

"Clean?

"Any STDs?"

"No. I'm clean."

"You won't die if we have sex?"

"If I do, I'll be dying and going to heaven."

"Best compliment a guy could give a girl. Now shut up and let me do this."

Molly lowered herself over Jack. She pushed the crotch of her panties aside as she guided him into her. She gasped as he filled her.

"Molly." His breath caught as she tightened around his cock. "Molly, it's my first time."

Molly couldn't believe her ears. Instantly, her body froze, and she glared at Jack. "What the hell? You're a virgin?"

"Yes. Is that so hard to believe?"

Molly scrambled off Jack. She picked up a pillow and threw it at him.

"Don't," he said as he caught it.

"You're lying," she said, reeling from the shock of Jack's admission. "There's no way you could be a virgin."

Jack zipped up his jeans and sat up on the couch. He winced as he felt his pants pull against his erection.

"It's not something I'd lie about. Is it so hard to believe that I haven't had sex yet?"

"Yes! When that person is you, the sexy lead singer in a famous band. That's what rock stars do—they bang their groupies; they have orgies on their tour bus; they get blown anytime they want. It's non-stop sex! Your dad's a hot movie star! Your name alone would get you into any girl's pants. There's no way you wouldn't take advantage of that. No way!" Molly huffed as she sat down heavily at the far end of the couch.

"Are you finished?"

"For the moment."

"You may be right about the sex lives of rock stars, and I'm flattered that you think I can have sex with any woman whenever I want, but I haven't slept with anyone. Ever. Call me funny, but I was waiting for the right woman."

"So, you're telling me I'm not the right woman for you? That's why you stopped me?"

"No. That's not what I'm saying. You are the right woman. I stopped you to tell you that."

"You don't have the right woman on an old leather couch in the office of a bar, Jack. It has to be more romantic than that."

"For me or you?"

"I don't know!"

"Where did you have your first time?"

Molly glared at him. "It's none of your damn business."

"I think it is. If I can tell you this would have been my first time, you should be able to tell me yours. Are you embarrassed?"

"I was disappointed in it. Not embarrassed."

"That bad, huh?"

"It was in my boyfriend's basement. We were babysitting his little brother. One thing led to another and it just kind of happened."

"Were you using birth control?"

"Yes. We used birth control. He had a condom he stole from his brother's wallet."

"Are you on something now?"

"I'm on the pill."

"Good, but you didn't ask me to wear a condom. Didn't you think I might have something if I've slept with hundreds of women? I might have lied to you."

"Don't worry, buddy, I won't make that mistake again," Molly fumed.

"Why are you mad at me?"

"Because!"

Jack got to his feet. "I'm sorry if my not having slept with hundreds of women bothers you. You wanted an experienced stud to rock your world. I think I would have done that, but now we'll never know. Thanks for a great night."

Jack headed for the door.

"Wait!" Molly called out to him. "Where are you going?"

"I'm heading back to my hotel. It's been a long day and contrary to other beliefs you may have about me I sleep alone." Jack opened the door and then turned to face her. "I don't need a king-sized bed, roses and soft music playing for my first time. I just knew it had to be you. And I like that couch."

Jack turned and left Molly totally and unbearably dumbfounded. She fell onto the couch, covered her eyes and groaned.

Jess opened the door within seconds of watching Jack leave the bar.

"What the hell happened? Did he take his shirt off?" she asked as she sat down on the couch and pulled Molly into her arms.

"I'm an idiot," Molly wailed.

"No, you aren't, honey. What happened?"

Jess rocked Molly in her arms, trying her best to comfort her best friend.

"I wanted him! Desperately."

"The bastard turned you down?"

"No! I ended up turning him down!"

"Why did you do that? Did he want to take his shirt off?"

"No. He's never taken his shirt off with anyone."

"What?"

"He's a virgin, Jess. He was saving himself for me, and I turned him down."

"You're messing with me. I've had a long day, Molly—"

"I'm serious, Jess. We started making out, and then he told me he was a virgin and I lost it. I couldn't go through with it."

"Why the hell not? Are you crazy?"

"He deserves better, Jess. He deserves a hell of a lot better."

five

Jack took his time walking back to his hotel. The band's tour bus had left once Axl, Ben and Matt had their fill of partying with their fans. Band rules made it clear that no one brought guests back to the hotel with them. Early in the tour, there had been some occasions where security had to remove an upset fan or two from Ben's and Axl's rooms. They lost points when that happened—lots of points.

The night air was cool. Jack cursed, realizing that in his rush to leave the bar, he had forgotten to take his jacket with him.

He knew he was an idiot to tell her he was a virgin, but he was laying it all on the line for her. She was honest with him. He thought it only fair to be honest with her. He thought he owed her that much after scaring the shit out of her with his tattoos. How else could he expect to get close to Molly if he didn't open up to her?

Jack felt no shame in keeping his virginity. He'd never felt the need to get laid. He didn't feel the need to live up to the reputation of a rock star. He saw first-hand the exploits of Axl and Ben and knew he wasn't missing anything special. Matt had a steady girlfriend waiting for him at home, and so he steered clear of getting into trouble.

Jack's dad, Quinn Thomas, had confided in Jack about his early sexual escapades when he first made it big in Hollywood. Without going into detail, Quinn told him sex was offered to him constantly.

He couldn't be in a woman's company without her offering him some sexual favour. It may have sounded like the perfect life, but Quinn couldn't handle the emptiness and loneliness that came with it. Once he found the love of his life, Jack's mom, she was it for him. They'd been together for twenty-five years.

He realized he had set his expectations high, but Jack didn't care. He wanted the perfect love from the beginning. He knew his soul mate was out there, and he was willing to wait for her.

Jack had heard the rumours about him being gay. When his twin sister, Stevie, came out as a teenager, people thought that he was gay, too—a cockeyed theory about twins inheriting the same gay gene fueled that rumour. Jack never denied or confirmed it. His sexuality was no one's business but his own.

The instant he saw Molly, Jack knew that she was the one. He'd seen her in his dreams, dreams of pleasure and torture all in one. At first, her appearance was sporadic. When he'd almost forgotten about her, she would come to him again and make love to him as only she could. Now, she haunted his dreams every night, promising she'd stay only to leave him alone clutching his pillow when the morning came.

He knew her mouth, the full lips and sweet taste of her kiss. When she kissed him tonight, his dreams became real. He knew she would torture him with her body, demanding more from him than he thought possible to give her. Jack smiled as he thought of her body, the small of her back when he led her to the dance floor, the fullness of her breasts when he held her close while they danced, and the sweet warmth of her when she guided his cock into her.

He would have made love to her on that couch. It didn't matter to him. Molly was all he wanted, and he would have done it right. In his dreams, she'd taught him how to love her, showed him how to please her. Jack knew in his heart that Molly would never have known that it was his first time, but he had to tell her, share with her how special she was to him. She wasn't an after-concert hook-up or points on the band's scorecard. She was his soul mate. He was sure of it. Now all he had to do was convince her of it.

six

Molly couldn't sleep. She tossed and turned in her bed, fearing that the ghosts from seventeen years ago would rear their ugly heads and haunt her dreams. Instead, Jack Thomas kept her awake. She wanted him. Her entire body ached for him. He may have been a virgin, but he knew all the right moves. Molly was sure of it. Her body tingled where he had touched her. Her lips ached for his kiss. She could feel the size of him as he entered her, if only for a brief moment.

"Idiot!" she called out in the darkness.

His last words to her haunted her, "I liked that couch." She squirmed underneath her sheets as she imagined lying naked beside him on that old leather couch. His lips covered hers as his hands caressed her body. She could feel the warmth move over her skin. She could feel the wetness grow between her legs. Molly groaned at the uncontrollable need to have Jack make love to her. She reached for the top drawer in her nightstand and pulled it open. She didn't need to turn on the light. She knew where everything was. Molly pulled out her favourite vibrator—the light purple one that glowed in the dark. There was no need for lubricant tonight. She was wet enough. Molly pressed the speed button and clicked it to low. Slowly, she inserted the vibrator into her vagina and arched against its invasion. Her arousal heightened; the lowest setting sent contractions throughout her body.

Images of Jack floated behind her closed eyelids. Jack in the tight leather pants and that oh so perfect ass. Jack soaking wet in the rain as water dripped from his dark mop of gorgeous hair. Jack covering her mouth with his as his breath touched her soul. Molly squeezed her breasts. He hadn't kissed her or touched her there. Her nipples were hard. She tweaked them with her fingers, gasping as the painful pleasure flowed through her. She cried out, wanting her hands to be his.

Not having Jack was torture. Molly wanted him, not this damned vibrator, but it would have to do. With a flick of a finger, Molly increased the vibrations. She pushed the vibrator further into her pussy, grinding it against her clitoris, forcing the quick release of her orgasm. Molly arched her back and cried out as she climaxed. It was a long release, long but unsatisfying.

She still ached for Jack. She cursed herself for turning him away. She hated herself for not being as understanding as she should have been. She damned the ghosts that came between them. Then she cried.

XO XO XO

Upon returning to his hotel room, Jack had a long hot shower. His brief encounter with Molly had left him hard. Visions of Molly flashed before him. Her long blonde hair, her full lips, and the way her ass moved just the right way when she walked filled his fantasy. He gripped his cock, and like so many times before, found relief. Minutes later, Jack fell into his bed tired and sated.

Jack woke to the sound of loud banging on his door. He tapped his watch, to find 3:00 a.m. illuminated on the time display. "Fuck off!" he yelled at the door.

"Jack! It's Molly. Open up!"

Jack scrambled out of bed wearing only boxer briefs. He unbolted the door and opened it. "Molly," he gasped, still half asleep. "What—"

She kept her eyes focused on the floor while she pushed her way past him to the king-sized bed. Molly kept her back to Jack.

"I hope you don't mind. This hotel is the only one in town, and I'm friends with the staff here. The night clerk gave me your room number."

Jack shook his head. "That's okay. Why are you here?"

"I can't sleep."

Jack shoved a hand through his mop of hair. "If it's about what happened—"

"I want you. I need to have you, Jack," she said as she undid her coat and dropped it to the floor.

"Molly, I don't think that's a good idea," he said while his gaze took in the sight of her bare bottom.

"Put on a shirt and let's make love."

"What? Why?"

"I behaved badly. I hurt you. I'm sorry," she said as her hands covered her face.

"You didn't. I'm not. You're forgiven," Jack stammered.

Molly took a deep breath then pushed back her shoulders. "Do you have a shirt on, or do you want to blindfold me?"

Whatever sleep his body craved was now forgotten. Jack's eyes opened wide as his cock jerked to attention at the suggestion. "Blindfold?"

"So, I don't see your tattoos."

Jack picked up the shirt he had bought at the bar from off the floor and sniffed it. It would do. He hurriedly pulled it over his head. "It's on."

Molly turned around. The red blotches on her face and her puffy eyelids told him she'd been crying for quite some time. Jack reached her in two strides. He took her in his arms and held her tight.

"Why were you crying?"

"It doesn't matter."

"Yes, it does. Tell me."

"It's the double rainbow."

"The rainbow?"

"Is it possible that the rainbow brought luck to both of us? Is that luck for us to be together?"

"Molly—"

"What if this is our chance to find love? What if I'm your soul mate, and you're mine? How can we ever be together if I can't bear to look at your tattoos?"

"I don't know. We don't have to come up with an answer now. We'll figure it out. I promise you." He kissed the top of her head to seal his promise.

Molly pushed out of Jack's embrace and led Jack to the bed. She lay down on the mattress and opened her arms to him. Jack accepted the invitation and lay down on his side facing her.

"You're beautiful," he said, awed by her nakedness.

"Kiss me."

Jack reached for Molly and pulled her to him. His mouth devoured hers, his tongue tasting all of her. He felt her soften in his arms, her moans encouraging him to continue kissing her, her fingers tugging on his hair giving him pleasure and pain. He'd been dreaming of her kisses and of the luscious lips that gave them.

When he finally released her from their kiss, Jack murmured softly to her, "I've been dreaming of this for a very long time. I've been dreaming of you, only you, my ladylove."

Molly gasped. His words caressed her heart, marking her soul. Before she could answer him, Jack moved down her neck, leaving hot kisses as he made his way to her breasts. He kissed each one tenderly, holding them in his hands as though they were a rare gift. His touch sent warm shivers through her body. His mouth took her nipple. Molly moaned as the pleasure flowed through her. He suckled her hungrily. His tongue flicked the hardened tip and then he nipped it softly. Everything Jack was doing to her was perfect, too perfect.

Molly pushed at Jack. "Stop!"

Jack looked up at Molly. "Am I doing something wrong?"

"You lied to me, Jack. You are not a virgin." Molly shoved her body away from him and sat up against the bed's headboard, pulling at a sheet to cover her breasts.

Jack gave his head a slow shake. "I don't lie." He exhaled heavily. "Damn it." He rolled to his back and stared at the ceiling.

"You're too good at everything you're doing to have not done it before. No one does it like that. Not without a lot of experience," she huffed, staring angrily at Jack. "I haven't had as many lovers as you, but I can tell."

"So, you think I'm good, do you?" A smile pulled at the corners of his mouth.

"You know you are. You played me, Jack Thomas."

He turned to face her, his gaze locking with hers. "I didn't play you if you meant I lied to you. But I do want to play your body as though it were a beautiful instrument because it is." Seeing the doubt in her eyes, Jack reached for Molly's hand. "I've never touched another woman. I swear to you. I know the mechanics of it. I just haven't used what I've learned."

"The way you touched my breasts—"

"Is there another way you'd prefer?"

"I love how you touched me. It's just that—"

"Trust me, Molly. There's been no one else." Jack moved to sit beside Molly.

"You're an anomaly, Jack."

"I've never been called that before. I've been called handsome, sexy, even gay, but never an anomaly." He chuckled softly.

"You're making fun of me."

"No, I'm not. I'm flattered that you think I've done this before."

"I'm making a mess of this, aren't I?"

Jack moved his arm behind Molly's shoulders and hugged her. "Nothing's messed up. It's all good. We're getting to know each other. We're learning to trust each other."

"How are you learning to trust me?"

"You're the only one, outside of my family to know I'm a virgin. I think that shows a hell of a lot of trust from a famous rockstar who has a certain image to protect."

Molly pulled back and looked up at Jack. She could see the honesty in his eyes. He didn't have to tell her he'd never had sex before, but he trusted her enough to confide his secret. And with that honesty came a smile that let her know that he wasn't the rockstar who slept around.

"Make love to me, Jack. I promise I won't stop you this time."

Jack loved her the way he had dreamed of loving her. With gentle hands and warm kisses, he played her body. Her moans and sighs were sweet music to his ears. His murmurs of pleasure added the bass line. Their hearts beat to their passion. When he finally entered her, they gasped in unison. Slowly, he moved in her, feeling her heat, feeling her hold him tight.

"You're my dream come true," he whispered to her, his sparkling blue eyes holding her gaze.

"Jack, I—"

She didn't have time to finish. Her orgasm exploded through her. She held on tight as Jack thrust harder, trying to catch up with her. Jack moaned his release before kissing her softly on the lips.

They lay there entwined. Jack nuzzled her neck, giving it warm kisses while Molly's soft hands caressed Jack's back beneath his sweat soaked shirt. Jack didn't move, surprised by her soft touch as she traced along his tattooed skin. He didn't dare disturb her, fearing her reaction once she realized she was touching him.

"This shirt is itchy," she said as her body relaxed beneath him.

"What do you expect? It's a twenty-dollar shirt," Jack grumbled.

"I think I'm going to break out in a rash," she complained, squirming away from him.

Jack frowned. "What if I get a rash? I'm the one who has to wear the damned shirt."

"Would you notice it?"

Jack gazed at her, trying to think of a smart-ass reply for her but couldn't. "I don't know," he finally answered her, "Other than the itch, I honestly don't know if I'd see it."

"Then keep the shirt on."

seven

Jack awoke, startled, at the sound of banging on his hotel door. His bed was empty. For a brief moment, he thought he had dreamed all last night until he felt the itch of the shirt. Jack stumbled out of bed, pulling on his jeans as he made it to the door.

"What?" he grumbled as he opened the door.

"Hey, Jacko, it's time for breakfast," Axl announced as he pushed by him. "You're usually up by now. What have you been doing?" he asked as he looked around the room and saw a woman's trench coat on the floor and ladies' boots by the bed. "You've got a hooker? You dog. Jealous of me and Ben collecting bonus points?"

Jack heard the sound of water running in the bathroom. "No, it's Molly. She's in the shower."

"The girl who ran out on you? Man, you must be desperate. I didn't think you'd see her again."

Jack heard the shower stop. Molly would be out soon, and she couldn't see Axl—tattooed Axl wearing a muscle shirt that exposed a lot of ink.

"You have to leave," he ordered him abruptly.

"Can't I meet her?" Axl asked, enjoying his friend's sudden embarrassment.

"Not now," Jack said as he opened the door, reinforcing the need for Axl to leave.

"I think I'll stay," Axl said, chuckling at his friend's discomfort as he dropped into the chair and made himself comfortable.

"Leave," Jack demanded. "She can't see you."

"Why not? You think she'll prefer me over you?"

Jack heard the lock on the bathroom door click.

"Fuck." Jack was stuck. Should he cover up Axl or throw Molly's coat at her in case she walked out of the bathroom naked? Quickly he grabbed Molly's coat and threw it at Axl. "Cover yourself."

The bathroom door opened wide showing Molly wearing the hotel's guest bathrobe. "Hello," she said slowly to Axl, noticing him sitting covered from the shoulders down with her trench coat.

"Molly, this is Axl, my best friend and the bass player of the band."

"Hi, Axl." Molly smiled, holding out her hand to him.

Axl tried to stand up, but Jack pushed him down.

"What gives, man?" he asked, surprised by his friend's behaviour.

"Molly, Axl's covered in tattoos. Do you mind staying in the bathroom so he can put on a shirt?"

"Oh." Molly's eyes opened wide. She stepped back into the bathroom and closed the door.

Axl looked up at Jack. "What was that all about?"

"She's terrified of tattoos. She can't look at them."

"You're kidding, right? You've got more than me."

"Mine are covered. Yours aren't. You have to leave. We'll see you at breakfast. Just put a shirt on with sleeves or wear a jacket. I'll explain everything later."

"You're banging a girl who's afraid of tattoos? Are you sick, man?" Axl asked, trying to suppress his laughter.

"Just go. Please."

Axl threw Molly's coat at Jack, before getting out of his chair and exiting the room. Jack closed the door behind him and leaned against it. He cursed, knowing that he would hear about this later. Axl, Ben and Matt would make sure they'd have a good laugh at Molly's expense. Molly was no laughing matter as far as he was concerned. He'd have to set them straight.

Jack called out to Molly, "He's gone."

Molly opened the door. "I'm sorry."

"It's not your fault. I told him we'd join him for breakfast."

"I can't. I'm already late for work."

"Will you come to tonight's concert? We're supposed to have a do over, remember?"

Molly shook her head. "I don't think that's a good idea."

Jack reached for her and pulled her toward him. He pressed his forehead to hers to meet her gaze. "I promise you. I won't take off my shirt. You'll see me just like I am now except that I'll be wearing a much nicer shirt, one that's not itchy."

"Hey! That's my merchandise you're dissing."

"I'll put you in contact with the band's marketing department. I'm sure we can get you a deal on a better-quality shirt."

"You promise?"

"About the shirt? Definitely."

Molly stuck her tongue out at him. "No, silly, the concert. Jack, I'm serious. I don't want to screw this up again."

"You won't. Promise me you'll come."

"Okay. I'll head back to the bar after the concert and wait for you there. Bring the band over for drinks, my treat."

"They'll like that."

Molly raised her chin to Jack, offering her mouth for a kiss. He didn't need encouraging. Molly clasped her arms around Jack's neck and pressed her body against his.

"Thank you," he murmured.

"For what?"

"For being the inspiration for my next tattoo."

XO XO XO

Molly stormed into her office, slamming the door so hard that the framed photographs on the wall rattled. She was still fuming, still outraged at the man who had pulled her in and played her like a fool.

"Virgin!" she yelled as she pulled off her coat and threw it on the floor as she made her way into her bedroom. She jerked on her underwear, pants, and a Maguire's T-shirt. "You're my dream come true," she sneered as she made her way to the bathroom. She grimaced while brushing out her hair and pulling it into a ponytail. "Trust me," she spat out as she reapplied her make up after she'd ruined it by crying all the way home from Jack's hotel room.

She didn't hear Jess entering the office or notice her standing in the bathroom doorway watching her. Molly turned around from the mirror and stopped when she saw her.

"How long have you been here?" she asked harshly.

"Enough to know that things didn't go well with the virgin rock star. Care to fill me in?"

Jess held out a steaming cup of coffee to her, knowing the magic effect caffeine had on Molly. It wouldn't take long for her to calm down. Molly accepted the offered brew, took a sip and walked out with Jess to the office.

"I wanted him, Jess. I went to him last night and begged him to make love to me. He was the perfect lover. He knew all the moves. It was like someone had given him a manual about me and he loved me in every way I'd ever dreamed about being made love to."

"So, why the tears?"

"Can a virgin know how to do that?" Molly cried out, still furious that she fell for that line.

"I don't know. You don't believe him?" Jess put down her coffee cup and took Molly's free hand in hers.

"I tried. I said I believed him. We talked about trust. How he trusted me enough to tell me he was a virgin and that I had to trust that he was telling the truth."

"So?" Jess squeezed Molly's hand.

"I thought we could be soul mates. Our connection, the way we looked at each other, the way we felt about each other." Molly took a deep breath and let it out in a long sigh. "Then I realized it was just me. He was letting me believe whatever I wanted. You were right. I was just another notch in his belt." Molly drained her coffee cup.

"Are you sure? He looked like he was totally into you last night."

"His father is Quinn Thomas! I'm sure he learned a few tricks from him, Jess."

"What did he say to you to get you this upset? It had to be something really bad."

"Jack told me I was the inspiration for his next tattoo. Can you believe it? He knows I'm terrified of them, and he's getting another one because of me!"

"It's like buying a pit bull for someone who's terrified of dogs," Jess said, knowingly.

"Exactly! So that's when I knew he played me. I told him to shove his tattoo and then I got the hell out of there."

"He didn't stop you?"

"He couldn't. I kneed him in the balls. He was on the floor when I left."

"You didn't!" Jess gasped. "Molly!"

"He deserved it."

"What if he was telling you the truth? You told me yourself his tattoos are of his family and everyone he loves. He could be really into you."

"What?" Molly asked as the possibility that she may have over-reacted sunk in.

"What if this tattoo he wants is a tribute to you, telling the world that you rocked his world? You did pop his cherry, Molly. That's a pretty big deal."

"Not to every guy."

"Maybe. So, what did you think it would be? Another notch in his belt? Does he have that kind of tattoo?"

"I don't know what he has! I won't look at them." Molly closed her eyes, remembering what Jack had told her. *Every drop of ink means something to me. Every picture reminds me of my family. Every tattoo pays tribute to someone I love.* Molly covered her face with her hands. "I'm a fool. He'll never come back. Not after what I did to him."

"If he's into you, he'll be back. I don't think a knee to the balls will stop him if he thinks you're the one," Jess's voice was calm and soothing.

Molly looked up at her. "Why are you so smart?"

"I'm the brunette, remember? Blondes need to have at least one brunette friend to keep them from completely fucking up their lives."

XO XO XO

Jack writhed in pain on the floor of his hotel room. As his breath and his senses gradually came back to him, he realized why Molly had reacted the way she had. His heart often spoke before his brain had the chance to step in. A tattoo for Molly? What was he thinking? Of course, he'd have one done for her, but to tell her now while she was still terrified of them and wouldn't even look at his? No wonder she'd hit and run.

Jack never thought she'd have a temper and react so quickly. He'd have to remember to wear a cup next time. That is if she'd give him another chance to talk to her. She was like him. Everything she did was from the heart. He knew that when he met her yesterday at the coffee shop. She saw the good in everything, except tattoos. He'd make her change her mind. He had to. It was all about trust.

"Finally," Axl exclaimed when Jack arrived at their table. "I thought maybe you and the tattoo girl decided to skip breakfast. Where is she?"

"Molly had to get to work."

Jack placed his breakfast order with their server. Axl watched her flirt with Jack. He saw the blush in her cheeks and the sensual lick of the lips. She'd probably do him at the table if Jack asked her to.

"What?" Jack asked when he noticed Axl giving him the look.

"You could have any woman you want, and you're going after someone who's terrified of you? I don't get it."

"It's not me. It's the tattoos. I told you. As long as I stay covered up, she's fine."

"You have to wear a shirt during sex?" Matt asked with keen interest.

"Or she wears a blindfold. Did you do that last night?" Ben asked.

"Let me know when you start using handcuffs. I want to hear all about it," Axl teased before he sipped his coffee.

"Seriously, guys, she's terrified of them. Her dad was killed by a guy covered in them. Molly was eight years old when she witnessed it. It still haunts her."

"That sucks," Matt said.

"So, does she think you're going to hurt her?" Ben asked in amazement.

"No, but the tattoos are like ghosts to her. That's what she calls them. They terrify the crap out of her. As long as I keep them covered, she's okay with me."

"That's weird shit, Jack, even for you," Axl said.

"She's worth it, Axl. She just has to learn to trust me."

eight

Molly tried to keep her mind off Jack. The busy Saturday afternoon crowd gave her little time to have a pity party. Jess wouldn't allow Molly to have one anyway because she was optimistic that Jack would make an appearance before his concert.

A huge crowd stood around the bar. The large screen televisions showing the baseball games made a good excuse for the male patrons to hover there. Jess knew they were ogling Molly, maybe her too, but most assuredly Molly. Molly smiled politely and filled their orders without her usual flirtatious banter. There was only one man she wanted to talk to—a man she might never see again.

Molly didn't notice the crowd part, making room for one more customer. However, Jess did and called out to Molly to take his order. Molly turned to find Jack leaning against the bar, smiling at her, oblivious to the attention he was getting from those gathering around him.

"You can walk," she said as she offered him a beer. "I'm sorry. What I did to you was below the belt."

"In more ways than one," Jack said, his gaze still riveted on her. "I figure I'm safe if I stay on this side of the bar."

"From me you are. I don't know if the ladies are going to leave you alone, though." Molly indicated the swarm of young women trying to get his attention.

"Can we talk in private?" he asked her. "I don't have much time."

"Sure." Molly nodded to Jess, who acknowledged her departure. Jess mouthed, "Good luck," to Molly.

Molly closed the office door behind them and leaned against it as she watched Jack take a seat on the couch.

"I didn't know if I'd see you again. I acted horribly."

"I jumped the gun. I should never have mentioned getting another tattoo."

"And I fired without asking questions," Molly added.

"You've got a fast knee. I guess you've done that before." He gestured toward her knees, exposed by her short black skirt.

"A few times, but usually I can talk a man into leaving before I have to resort to that. I also have a baseball bat on the wall behind the bar."

"I'll remember that."

Molly walked over to Jack. She gazed down at him and reached for his hair. She loved the feel of it, running her fingers through the thick brown strands. "Last night was incredible."

"I know," his voice was soft and warm, sending shivers through her.

"Are you sure you've never done anything like that before?"

"I think I'd remember it if I had." He smiled. "You still don't believe me?"

"You make it hard to, but I'm trying."

Jack reached for Molly and pulled her onto his lap. "How can I convince you that you are the only one?" His eyes searched her face for understanding, desperately needing her to trust him.

"Kiss me," she murmured.

Jack kissed her, pulling her in close to him, holding her as though his very existence depended on it. Molly responded to him by kissing him harder, deeper. Her hands cupped his face, keeping his mouth on hers. They both moaned softly, feeling the heat pulse through them.

"I have to go," Jack groaned as he forced himself to pull away from her. "We have interviews scheduled at the auditorium. The band's going to be on television."

"Why did you come?"

"To make sure you'd forgiven me and to make sure you'd come to the concert tonight."

"I didn't hear an apology," Molly said before she kissed him again.

"I'm sorry."

"Show me." Molly pushed back from him. "Let's try this again," she said as she unzipped her skirt and let it fall to the floor.

"Did I tell you how much I liked this couch?" The bulge in his jeans showed her how much.

Molly undid Jack's zipper and released his cock. She straddled him, pulled the crotch of her panties aside, and guided him into her. His hands gripped her hips.

"Let me do all the work, Jack. Just enjoy. It's your turn."

"I enjoyed last night and this morning," he said, smiling. He leaned back against the couch and kept his gaze focused on her. There was none of the slow lovemaking or foreplay they shared earlier. Molly moved with a deliberate pace as she rode him.

"There are some things you should know about me. I have a quick temper."

"I gathered that," Jack answered as he tried to concentrate on what she was saying and not what she was doing to him.

"I'll admit it when I'm wrong, but I rarely am."

"Okay." Jack grimaced as he tried to hold back his orgasm. He was coming too fast.

"And when I'm wrong but won't admit it, it's still your fault. Got it?"

Her mouth came down hard on his. Molly kissed the life out of him and cleared his brain of all rational thought. Jack struggled to remember what her question was. It didn't matter. He would agree to anything for her.

"Yes," he groaned as the last of his concentration shattered. His fingers dug into the soft flesh of Molly's thighs as he came hard and fast.

Molly threw her head back and cried out. She shuddered as her orgasm tore through her. After a moment, Molly leaned forward and took Jack's face in her hands and kissed him tenderly. "One more thing," she added.

"Anything."

"No blonde jokes. Only Jess can make fun of me being blonde. One blonde joke and you're on the couch. Alone."

"I don't like blonde jokes," Jack assured her. "Never have. Never will."

Molly slipped off his lap, picked up her skirt and then walked to the office bathroom.

Jack sat staring at the ceiling as he fastened his jeans. "So does this mean we're dating?"

Molly poked her head around the door. "Dating?"

"Well, I'm kind of new to this, so I want to make sure I don't have my signals crossed."

"You've dated before, Jack Thomas. Don't give me that bullshit."

He smiled at her. "I haven't dated you before. I want to get this right with you, Molly Maguire."

"I'll have to think about it."

"What's there to think about?"

"Do I want to settle for a night of hot sex, or do I want to devote days, weeks or months of trying to have a relationship with you despite you being a tattooed rock star who is on the road with thousands of groupies throwing themselves at you every day?"

"That's a tough decision, but I know which one I'd choose." Jack got to his feet and walked toward Molly. "Date me. I promise to give you more hot sex, and I won't even look at a groupie." He put his hand on his chest over his heart. "Scout's honour."

Molly laughed. "You were never a boy scout, Jack."

"Date me and you'll find out."

She couldn't look away from him. The sincerity reflected in his eyes told her that he was worth the effort.

"Okay. We'll date." Molly stepped back into the washroom, leaving the door slightly ajar.

"Don't you want to know anything about me?" he asked from behind the door.

"What do I need to know?"

"I fart."

"Everyone farts, Jack. It's not a big deal."

"I like to fart on stage. I get Axl all the time when we're performing. I walk over to him when he's playing, and I just let it rip, and then I walk away."

Molly opened the door so that she could look at him. "You're proud of that?"

"Not particularly, but it's worth 10 points. Fifty if it fucks up his playing."

"What?"

"Never mind. I'll tell you about it later."

"Do you fart in bed?"

"No."

"Good, because if you fart in bed when I'm with you, you'll be on the couch. Alone."

"Will the couch always be my punishment?" Jack asked as he gazed at the couch. "Because I like this couch." He turned his attention back to her and smiled.

Molly couldn't take her eyes off him. Damn he was sexy when he smiled at her that way with his messy hair, sparkling blue eyes, and the body that promised great sex. Molly stepped toward him. "I have to work, and you have interviews to get to."

"I can be late," he said as he tucked a stray blonde hair behind her ear.

"I can't. Jess is waiting on me." Molly nodded to his crotch. "Can you save that for later?"

"Rain check?" Jack asked her before he kissed her mouth softly.

"Definitely a rain check," Molly murmured against his lips.

XO XO XO

Molly knowingly dressed for the concert. She wanted Jack's eyes only on her. She didn't just want to be the pretty girl in the audience who dated Jack Thomas. She wanted to be the woman who drove him wild with desire. She wanted him to know that she desired him, too, and that he was hers.

Molly felt that all eyes were on her when she walked down the aisle to her seat. She heard the whispers behind her back from those who recognized her as the bartender from across the road who always wore a Maguire's black T-shirt and jeans. Tonight, she was dressed in killer skin-tight black leather pants that stopped inches below her navel, a black lace bustier that showed more than it covered, and Jack's black leather jacket. Jack wouldn't see the five-inch stiletto heels until later in a sex-filled fantasy she planned to share with him after the concert. Molly let her hair fall freely past her shoulders. She had applied a light cover of makeup, making sure her lips were an eye-catching red. No one knew she was the lover of the man they all came to hear. She liked that.

Molly sipped her beer slowly, enjoying the banter she heard from various female fans of Dragon Slayers. There were those who were infatuated with the bass player, Axl, but most were lovesick over Jack.

"What I wouldn't do to have ten minutes with Jack Thomas. I'd rock his world, and he'd be mine forever," a female fan yelled at her friend over the rising noise from the audience.

"Five minutes," her friend yelled back at her. "He'd be mine in five. On his knees and begging for more."

"Two minutes," Molly yelled out to them, only to have her words drowned out by cheers when the lights began to dim.

The announcer yelled over the sound system, "All the way from Toronto, Canada, Dragon Slayers!"

The women shrieked and ran to the stage. Molly sat still as she waited for Jack to make his way to centre stage. She timed it perfectly. As Jack took his position, Molly stood up and pulled off Jack's jacket. Jack saw her at once, surprise and lust combined in one heated gaze. She smiled at him as she made her way through the crowd. The crowd parted as though they knew something big was about to happen. Molly walked to the edge of the stage and held out his jacket to him. It was the least she could do. He had promised her he'd stay covered up for the concert. She'd stay uncovered for him.

Jack leaned down and kissed Molly, then straightened and brought the jacket to his face and inhaled her scent. He hardened instantly. He smiled when she blew him a kiss, then watched her wiggle her ass as she made her way back to her seat.

"Jack!" their manager shouted at him through his earpiece. "Are you going to sing or just watch that piece of ass all night? We've got a show to do. Get going!"

Jack pulled on his jacket and then nodded toward the sound booth. "One, two, three, four!" he called out.

The concert began.

Jack gave the best performance of his life. He had the audience in the palm of his hand. They loved every song, every story he told them, and every move he made on stage. They didn't know he was playing for one woman only—she did. Her gaze never left him. She caught the smile he sent her way and saw the sparkle in his eyes when he talked about love's first kiss. She could feel her heart beat fast when he spoke of his newfound love. She melted when he sang to her.

Then it happened.

The audience started to chant, "Take it off. Take it off. Take it off!"

Jack shook his head no. He tried to ignore the crowd and sing the next song. Unfortunately, it was the song he was known for taking off his shirt to show off his tattoos. Jack cursed under his breath as he realized the crowd wasn't going to stop their frenzied chanting.

Molly looked around her as fear started to tear at her insides. The women around her were stripping off their T-shirts and waving them over their heads, screaming, demanding that Jack strip, too. Then two men from the audience rushed down to the front of the stage. They were shirtless, and their tattoo-covered torsos blocked Molly's view of the stage. Molly looked away from them only to see their grotesque images on the giant screens hanging from the rafters.

The ghosts were back, and they were screaming for her. Molly squeezed her eyes shut as she recited her mantra, "It's only a tattoo. It will not hurt me. It was a man who killed my father, not a tattoo. There is nothing to fear. It's only a tattoo!" Images of her father's murder flashed before her. She covered her eyes with her hands, desperate to keep the ghosts away. Molly's ears rang from the deafening roar of the crowd.

"Take it off!" the crowd chanted.

Jack watched Molly. She hadn't run away, although she was bent over in her seat with the palms of her hands pressed to her eyes. This concert was going to be the end of her, and it was going to be the end of them if he didn't do something now.

Jack rushed forward to the security guards who were trying to keep the tattooed men back from the stage. "Get them out of here," he yelled. "I don't care what you have to do but get them the hell out of here!" Jack turned to face Axl and yelled, "Molly's Rain."

He did the same to Ben and Matt, then picked up his acoustic guitar and started to play. Jack waited for the crowd to hear the music. He waited for their silence and the sanity to resume before he sang to her.

"She sat by the window staring at the rain,
She said rain brings good luck you know.
It washes away the bad, washes away the pain."

Molly heard his voice. He was singing to her, telling her everything was okay. He was telling her to trust him. The ghosts were gone. Molly wiped away her tears and looked at Jack. She could see the fear in his face and hear the love in his voice. Molly smiled and blew Jack a kiss. It was the best she could do. She hadn't run. For the first time, Molly hadn't run.

nine

Molly listened to her office speakerphone while her mother lectured her from hundreds of miles away. "Molly, be reasonable here. You're asking for trouble and a broken heart."

"Mom," Molly groaned, exasperated by her mother's unwillingness to let her have the chance to speak.

"No, Molly, you listen. How many years did you go through therapy, trying hypnosis or anything under the sun that we thought would help you?" She didn't let Molly answer. "Too many to count, Molly, that's how many. I'm not going to sit back and watch you set yourself up for major heartbreak and more emotional trauma. It's a pity that young man decided to mark himself in that way. Each to his own, I guess. Can't you find someone who doesn't have tattoos?"

"I didn't know he had tattoos, Mom. But I want to try."

"Try what? To have a normal relationship when you can't look at him with his clothes off? Tell me, Molly, how long do you think he'll be willing to put up with this? How long did it last with the last man who had tattoos?"

"Mom," Molly winced, realizing she couldn't win this argument.

"Five days until the novelty had worn off for him. Sweetheart, find someone else. Someone you can love completely. Not someone you can only love conditionally."

"Mom, we just met. I shouldn't have told you about him."

"You cannot love him and his tattoos no matter how hard you try. Give up this foolish idea about having a relationship with this man and end it now."

"He's on tour, Mom. I don't know when I'll see him again, but if he wants to see me, I won't say no. I like him."

Molly's mother sighed heavily. There was a long awkward silence between them before she spoke again. "You're old enough to decide for yourself. You don't know how much I wish I had taken you shopping with me that day. Then you wouldn't be so terrified of—"

"Tattoos," Molly finished for her.

"Then you could be happy with anyone you wanted to love. This man, no matter how much you want to look past his markings, he'll always have them. They'll always come between you."

"Always is a long time."

"I know," her mother agreed.

"I'm going to try, Mom. I didn't run tonight. I told you that."

'Yes, but it's when you stay and keep your eyes open that matters. How long do you think it will take before that happens?"

Once again, an uncomfortable silence came between them. Molly didn't let it last for long. It was time to change the subject. "I'm feeling better now. The antibiotics seem to have worked."

"That's good, sweetie," her mother's voice was instantly warm and comforting. "It's important to stay healthy when you're working around so many people and their germs."

Molly smiled at her mother's comment. Her mother never felt at ease being around strangers all of the time. It was one of the reasons why she was eager to leave the bar to Molly. Molly loved being around people.

"I have to go, Mom. Jack should be here soon. I invited his band over for drinks."

"I love you, Molly."

"Love you too, Mom," Molly said with a touch of sadness.

XO XO XO

After the concert, Jack and the band eventually made their way to Maguire's. They had more interviews with the press and fans who needed pictures taken with them before the foursome could finally call it quits and leave the auditorium.

Jess waved to Jack when they entered the bar and pointed to a reserved table. While they were settling in their seats, Jess came over to them carrying a tray of beer and three liquor bottles. She set the tray in the middle of the table.

"Is she okay?" Jack asked before he made the introductions.

"She's fine. She's in her office talking to her mom on the phone. It's her Saturday night ritual."

Jess turned her attention to the other three men at the table. "Hello there. My name's Jess. I'll be your bartender tonight. The drinks are on the house, and food's coming."

"Jess, this is Ben, our drummer, Matt plays guitar and keyboards, and the creepy guy staring at your chest is Axl."

"Well, hello, Jess, nice to meet you."

"You must be the bass player," Jess said as she held out her hand to Axl. "You rock that dark side look."

Axl laughed heartily. "Jack, I love this woman even though we've just met."

"Easy there, man, no scaring off the bartender until we've had at least another three rounds!" Ben warned.

Jack read the labels of the liquor bottles. "Don't I need a glass for the Jack Daniels? If that's Molly's drink of choice I should get used to it."

Jess sat down on the chair beside him. "You're a sweetheart, Jack, but you need to know the facts of life where Molly's drinks are concerned if you're going to date her."

She looked him straight in the eyes. "Are you planning on dating Molly?"

"Yes."

"Good answer. Now listen carefully."

Jack arched his eyebrow, curious to know what Jess had to tell him about liquor. Jess was an attractive woman, not much older than Molly. She kept her brunette hair styled in a bob that complimented her face. Her eyes were an intense green that demanded she received his full attention.

Jess pointed to the bottle of Jack Daniels. "Molly only drinks this when she sees the ghosts. It was her dad's drink of choice and for a reason only known to Molly, this is the only drink that will calm her. It usually takes about a fifth of a bottle before it kicks in."

"Mind if we listen in? In case Jack forgets?" Matt asked.

Jack shrugged his approval. "How often does she see the ghosts?" Jack asked before taking a swig of his beer.

"She's pretty good at avoiding them. It's like she's got a sixth sense and knows when to turn away." Jess laughed and cocked her head at Jack. "Although she didn't see you coming."

"When was the last time she reacted badly?" Jack had to know if this was a regular occurrence.

"About a year ago some idiots got drunk and decided to strip and do a table dance at the same time. It was too much for her, especially seeing them in here." Jess sighed. "I think she finished the bottle that night." She pointed to Jack's beer. "If she's drinking this everything is right with her world, got it?"

"Got it," Jack nodded.

"White wine's for when she's feeling sexy."

"Feeling sexy?" Jack gave her his mischievous grin.

"When she needs a man, Jack." Jess laughed at the expression on his face.

Jack looked thoughtful before he asked, "How often does she drink white wine?"

"I said when she needs a man, not when she takes one, Jack. Molly looks after herself in that department, if you know what I mean."

"Oh," Jack said and pointed to the vodka cooler. "What about the cooler?"

"Offer her a cooler and you're bound to get hit with the bottle without her taking a sip. It has to do with bad high school memories and blonde jokes. It's all I can do to get her to sell this shit in the bar. The female college students love the stuff."

"So, you and Molly are close?" Jack asked her, already knowing the answer.

"Like sisters," Jess replied. "We have each other's back."

Jess gave Jack a once over. He was gorgeous. There was no doubt about it. Nothing about him needed improvement except for his tattoos for Molly's sake. The way he smiled at her made her want to trust him.

"Don't hurt her," she warned him. "She's falling for you. No one should fall this fast or hard for someone, but I know she's falling for you."

"I've fallen for her, Jess. It hit us both."

"What's hit us both?" Molly asked when she arrived at their table.

"You and me falling for each other," Jack said as he stood up to greet her. "How are you? I'm sorry about what happened." He gazed down at her with concern.

"I stayed. For the first time, I didn't run."

"I wouldn't have blamed you if you did." He sighed as he pulled her in close for a hug. Images of the tattooed goons flashed before his eyes.

Molly felt him tense. "It's okay. It's over. I'm good." She looked down at the three men sitting at the table. "Hey, guys."

"Molly, I'd like you to meet Ben and Matt. You and Axl met this morning. Ben and Matt, this is Molly."

"I've got to get back to the bar. See you guys later," Jess said, getting to her feet. "Your nachos will be here soon." She picked up the tray of liquor bottles and took them with her.

"Can we have them to go?" Ben asked.

Molly looked at Jack.

"I didn't get the chance to tell you that our bus leaves in a few minutes. We've been asked to add on a few more radio interviews. I'm sorry."

"You're heading out?" Molly asked in surprise. She could feel a knot in her stomach. "Of course, you are," she said as she shook her head. "You're on tour."

Jack cursed under his breath. The last thing he wanted to do was upset Molly. Tonight, they should be celebrating that she made it through the concert. They should be hanging out with the guys, letting them get to know her and see why she was special to him. Instead, they would only see her as the crazy hot chick who owned a bar.

"Hey, it's only for two weeks," Axl chimed in. "I'm sure you won't forget what Jack looks like. I mean who could forget those tats."

Jack's eyes narrowed as he gave Axl the sign to shut up. He didn't need him messing things up for him and Molly.

Jack caressed Molly's cheek. He loved the softness of her skin and the way she closed her eyes and smiled at his touch. "I don't want to leave you. Not after I just found you."

"I'll still be here," Molly reassured him. "I'll always be here."

"I'll call you every day. So much that you'll get sick of me."

"I doubt that," Molly replied. "I love the sound of your voice."

They all heard the blast from the tour bus's horn.

"We have to go," Jack announced.

"Where's our nachos?" Ben asked.

Axl got to his feet. "Another time, Ben. I'm sure we'll be passing by this way soon. Come on. Let's give these two a minute to say good-bye."

He gave Molly a big hug, stepped back and let Ben and Matt do the same.

"Nice meeting you, Molly," Ben said cheerfully.

"Yes. Good to meet you," Matt agreed.

Jack nodded his appreciation to his bandmates.

"Kiss me," Molly said when she turned to him. "Make it last me for two weeks."

"Ah, Molly," Jack moaned as his mouth covered her sweet lips with a long hot kiss. He didn't want this to end. He could feel her hold tighten on his heart, and he ached to stay with her. "I'll be back. I promise."

"I'll be waiting."

ten

Axl made his way to the front of the bus, away from those who were trying to sleep. He found Jack sitting in a leather chair with his legs sprawled out in front of him, one bare foot tapping out a beat, while he played his acoustic guitar.

"Can't sleep?" he asked Jack as he sat down on the leather couch across from him.

"I've got this song running through my head. I can't let it go."

"Another gift from your muse?"

Jack didn't answer until he finished playing. "I can't stop thinking about her. It's as though she's opened up something deep inside. I've got all this music flowing out of me."

"Have you got lyrics for that?" Axl nodded his head toward the notebook on the floor by Jack's chair.

"Yes, but I think you'll come up with something better." Jack reached for his notebook and tossed it to Axl.

"You mean that don't you?" Axl asked while he glanced at Jack's scrawl.

"Of course, I do. You've got the gift for lyrics, man. You've always had it."

Axl straightened. "Whoa, what brought this on? You've never told me that."

"There are a lot of things I haven't told you. There's some stuff going on in my life that I'd like to share with you, but I can't. Not yet."

"You're my best friend, Jack. I think of you as my brother. You know you can tell me anything, and it won't leave this bus."

"I know, but I made a promise that I can't break. I'm sorry."

"It has to do with the band, doesn't it?" Axl demanded.

"What makes you think that?"

"We've all heard the rumours. After this tour, you're ditching us to go solo."

"Don't listen to rumours, Axl. You know better than that."

"Swear on your mom's life that you're not ditching the band."

"What?"

"You heard me," Axl ordered him. "Swear on your mom's life that you're not leaving the band and I'll believe you."

Jack's eyes burned with anger. He could feel the heat in his cheeks. "You're fucking crazy if you expect me to do that. If you don't believe me, then you can go to hell."

"Fuck you," Axl yelled as he got to his feet and stormed off to his bunk at the back of the bus.

Jack sat back in his chair, reeling from Axl's outburst. "What the hell?"

They were best friends, brothers without the blood tie. Jack couldn't remember a time when Axl wasn't in his life. Friends since elementary school, bandmates since they both got their first guitar. It ate at Jack that he couldn't confide in Axl, but he'd made a promise, and he'd never break that trust.

XO XO XO

Jess walked into the bar office to find Molly hunched over the laptop on her desk. A pot of coffee, a box of chocolates and used tissues covered the desk. Molly looked up at Jess with bloodshot eyes, puffy from too much crying, and mascara smudges. She had her hair pulled back in a messy ponytail, with more hair hanging loose than tied back. Jess made a mental note to herself to get Molly waterproof mascara and a headband next time she went to the drugstore.

"What's up?" she asked, trying to act casual.

Molly sniffed and wiped her nose. "I'm trying to watch Jack's videos. I want to be able to look at his tattoos without freaking out."

"Any luck?" Jess asked, already knowing the answer.

"Is there one video of him without him stripping? For Pete's sake, he sings and shows skin. It doesn't matter what the song is about; he's always showing off those damned tattoos!"

Jess sat on the desk and looked at the laptop screen. The band's latest video was playing, and Jack was visible in all of his tattooed glory. Jess whistled her appreciation. "He is gorgeous, Molly. Those tattoos don't hide that at all."

"Jess!" Molly whined. "You're not helping."

"Sorry! Did you manage to watch any of these?"

"I think ten seconds is the longest I can watch. I was hoping that he'd only show his arms in one so I could get used to him bit by bit, but there's nothing like that." Molly closed the laptop screen. "I've got two weeks to get my shit together. What if I can't look at him when his tour is over?"

"Did he give you an ultimatum?" Jess asked horrified.

"No! I gave it to myself. It's not fair to string him along if I can't fix this!"

Jess put her hand on Molly's shoulder. "Hon, you've been trying to get over this fear of tattoos for seventeen years. What makes you think you can fix it in two weeks?"

"Love?" Molly asked, too tired and mentally exhausted to answer with conviction.

"You met him two days ago. Don't you think love's a bit strong?" Jess cringed when she heard the words coming from her mouth. Sometimes it sucked being the rational friend.

Molly's bloodshot eyes opened wide. "Maybe it's not love, but I like him. I really like him. He likes me, too."

"Then he'll understand if you're not quite ready for him in two weeks time. How long have you been watching his videos?" Jess guessed she'd been up all night by the way Molly looked. "Don't bother answering. It doesn't matter," she muttered.

Molly yawned while rubbing her tired eyes, smearing whatever mascara remained into dark circles under her eyes.

Jess couldn't help but smile. "Okay, Molly raccoon eyes, it's time for you to hit the shower and go to bed." Jess stood up and offered Molly her hand. "Don't bother arguing with me and don't bother coming out until you've had at least six hours of beauty rest. You'll scare the customers away if they see you looking like that."

Molly, too tired to resist, let Jess lead her into the bedroom adjoining the office. "I'll shower when I wake up," Molly mumbled as she opened the door to her bedroom and headed for her bed.

"Sweet dreams," Jess cooed as she tucked her friend into bed.

They came back. Molly hadn't dreamed about them in months, and now the ghosts had come back to torment her with a vengeance. The dream started the same as it always had for the past seventeen years. Molly was in the bar playing while her father polished the beer glasses. Then the tattooed man appeared, hovering over her father and shouting at him. Molly covered her ears to block out the sound. Visions of the slashing knife, the blood, and her father's crumpled body flashed before her quickly followed by the crazed murderer's face. He started toward her. Molly couldn't look away from him. She recognized the brilliant blue eyes, the shaggy brown hair, and the mischievous smile, and then she screamed.

eleven

After Jack showered on the bus, he downed a couple of cups of strong coffee to prepare for a day filled with countless press interviews. He thought of Molly and wanted to call her, but he knew it was too early. He wondered if she had dreamed about him through the night. He ached to tell her how much she was on his mind.

They arrived in San Francisco just in time for the live interview on one of the morning radio talk shows. He and Axl hadn't exchanged one word since their conversation a few hours earlier. Jack didn't have the energy to deal with Axl and his allegations. No matter how much he was pissed at Axl for wanting him to swear on his mother's life, Jack knew that the tour and the band came first. He'd learned from his dad at an early age that there was a Hollywood face for the public and a real face for your friends and family. Fans always deserved to see the best side of their idols, not the worst.

"Let me talk this time," Axl snapped at Jack when they arrived for their first interview of the day.

Jack held up his hands as he surrendered the chair closest to the interviewer to Axl. He hoped Axl would remain professional during the interview and not air his grievance with Jack. He wasn't disappointed. Once Axl started to speak for the band, he proved that the rough and tough looking bass player was a talkative and funny guy. Ben, being the shy and quiet type, stayed true to form and let the others do the talking. Matt offered a comment or two about their music and mentioned that he had a girlfriend.

During their last interview on a popular San Francisco alternative radio station, Jack wasn't allowed to sit back and let Axl answer the questions. The controversial and opinionated radio host made it known to everyone that he was not going to give the standard interview.

"Jack, you've been very evasive when it comes to your sexuality. When are you going to come clean with your fans?"

Axl, Ben and Matt laughed into their microphones.

Jack gave the interviewer his best smile. "I don't think I've been evasive at all. No one has ever asked me, and quite frankly, it's no one's business."

"But surely, you'll agree that you have hundreds of thousands, perhaps millions of female fans who fantasize about you. They call themselves the Slain, don't they? Don't you think it's cruel of you to lie to them? Shouldn't you put your fans first and just come out of the closet?"

"Oh man," Axl said into his microphone. "You are so—"

"I'm straight." Jack's tone was hard as steel, just like his eyes. "I know there are rumours about me. Probably because my twin sister came out when she was a teenager and people like yourself assume that if one twin is gay, the other one has to be. Well, that's simply not true."

"You've never been seen with a woman."

"I must be good at avoiding the paparazzi."

"A trick you learned from your father? He was quite the ladies' man. Are you anything like him?"

Jack kept his cool. One thing he had learned from being around his father during press junkets for his movies was never let the interviewer get the best of you no matter how much of an ass they were.

"I hope I am like my father. To be compared to him is quite the compliment."

"Do you care to elaborate?"

"No."

"Are you seeing anyone?"

"What's with the interrogation?" Ben asked. "We're here to talk about our music, not about the crazy bartender chick Jack's banging."

Matt let out an audible gasp, while both Axl and Jack stared at Ben in disbelief as to why their shy drummer suddenly chose this moment to speak out.

"What?" Ben asked when the room became awkwardly silent. "You're a dick," he said pointing at the radio host, "and Jack, buddy, you've got serious shit to work out with tattoo girl to make a go of it. Now can we please talk about our music?"

✗o ✗o ✗o

"What the hell went on in there?" Jack shouted at his bandmates once they were in the privacy of their limousine. "Ben, you crossed the line. No personal stuff, remember? Dragon Slayers only."

"Oh, that's sweet coming from you," Axl sneered.

"Something had to be said," Ben explained. "The interview was off the rails because your head is so far up your ass right now all you say is bullshit."

"Like hell it is," Jack snapped.

"Then for once be straight with us. Tell us what's going on with you. Why do you disappear after every concert? Are you meeting with another label? Are you planning to go solo?"

"We've got a right to know, Jack," Matt agreed.

"Why can't you just trust me when I say that I'm not leaving?"

"We're brothers, man. Brothers don't have secrets," Axl said.

Jack shoved his hands through his hair and cursed. "Damn it, I made a promise."

"Trust in us to keep the secret. Have we ever let you down?" Axl asked.

Jack shifted in his seat. "My mom's been fighting cancer. She didn't want anyone outside of the family to know about it because of the way the press handled her last cancer scare. She lost all privacy, and you know how much she wants to keep her private life private."

"We wouldn't have said anything," Ben said.

"I know, but she made all of us promise."

"How is she?" Matt asked.

"She finished her last round of radiation this week. Dad says she'll be fine."

"That sucks about your mom, bro. She's always been a fighter. Good to hear she's kicking cancer's ass this time around, too."

"What about your after-concert departures?" Axl reminded him.

"Phone calls to my mom. I've been having these dreams. She's the only one I can talk to about them. It's just the right time to reach her when she's by herself. Dad freaks out when he hears us talking about our dreams."

"What kind of dreams?" Matt asked.

"I've been dreaming about the dragon again."

His friends had heard the stories about Davina Thomas' kidnapping and shooting. Both of them knew that her family referred to her battles with cancer as fighting the dragon. They also knew the story behind Jack's tattoos and supported the idea of calling their band Dragon Slayers. They had dragon tattoos, too, but nothing that matched Jack's.

"What's the dragon up to this time?" Ben asked.

"Damned if I know."

XO XO XO

"You were supposed to sleep," Jess admonished Molly when she joined her at the bar. Jess knew the drill. Let the first cup of caffeine course through Molly's veins before asking her what was going on in that blonde head of hers. It wouldn't help anyone to press her now. Jess made herself look busy as she worked around Molly's statue-like body as she stared out at the customers.

Molly ignored Jess, pretending she couldn't hear her over the coffee machine while she made an Americano coffee for herself. The only thing that moved was Molly's arm as she brought the coffee cup to her lips.

"The ghosts came back," Molly whispered. "They wouldn't let me sleep."

"Damn it, Molly!"

Molly looked at Jess with quiet terror in her eyes. "This time, it was Jack's face. Every one of them had Jack's face."

"It's those music videos you were watching all night. They stayed with you."

"I know."

Jess wrapped her arm around Molly's waist. "So that plan didn't work. We'll have to think of something else," she said, trying to reassure Molly.

"No."

"Why?" Jess turned to look at her.

"Because I realize that no matter how many pictures of Jack I look at, I won't be able to look at him in the flesh. If I can't handle glimpses of his tattoos on my computer, what makes me think I can ever look at them when I'm with him?"

"So, you're giving up?"

"I'm giving in to you and my mom. Both of you are right. It's madness to think I can get over what seventeen years of therapy haven't accomplished."

"I thought he might have been the one."

Molly shook her head. "I did, too. Maybe it's one of those crash and burn romances that lasts for a moment in time. It was amazing, but now I know it was foolish to think it could last."

"Does Jack know?"

"Not yet. He's texted me a few times. I don't have the heart to answer him. I need more coffee before I can do that."

XO XO XO

Jack looked at his watch. It was half-past three in the afternoon. No wonder he was hungry. They hadn't stopped to have a bite to eat since they started this morning. He was still pissed at Ben for his outburst during their last interview. Ben had no right to say anything about Molly. Jack's personal life was private. To make matters worse, Molly hadn't replied to any of his voicemails or texts. Jack stepped out of the elevator and headed to his room.

Once inside his hotel room, Jack stripped, before placing a call to room service for a burger and fries. When finished, Jack picked up his cell phone and pressed speed dial.

"Jack," a woman's husky voice answered after the second ring. "It's been a while. What's up? Did you miss me?"

"Of course, I missed you. I'm in San Francisco. I have a couple of hours free. Can you stop by?"

"I'll have to cancel my afternoon appointment with one of my regulars," she answered. "It will cost you."

"It always does. I'm staying at The Hilton, room 1610. Thanks, Harley."

Jack walked into the bathroom for a quick shower. By the time he was dressed, room service had arrived with his order. Jack sat in one of the large armchairs and dialed Molly's number on his cell phone.

She answered on the fourth ring. "Hello?"

"Molly. Hi, it's Jack. How are you? I've been trying to reach you."

His warm voice caressed her, and her knees weakened as she remembered the taste of his kiss and the pleasure his mouth gave her. She mouthed his name to Jess before she left for the privacy of her office.

"Molly? Are you there?"

"Yes, Jack," she stammered. "I'm heading to my office. It's too noisy in the bar."

"I've missed you. I can't believe it's only been a few hours since I last saw you."

"Where are you?"

"San Francisco. We play here tonight and then we're off to Portland. I have a couple of hours before we head out for our sound check. I had to hear your voice."

"Oh."

"So, how's the weather today in Ingledale? Any more freak thunderstorms?"

"Not today."

"Molly, is something wrong? You don't sound like yourself."

"I'm fine."

There was a knock at Jack's door. "I have to go. Can I call you tonight? It will be late, but I need to talk to you."

"Jack, I run a bar. I'll still be up."

The call went dead. Jack looked at his cell phone as though it would explain to him what just happened. Something wasn't right.

Once again, there was a knock at the door. Jack tossed his cell phone onto the bed and answered the door.

"Hey, gorgeous, how are you?" a black-haired beauty asked as she sauntered into the room, pulling her wheeled case behind her.

"I want something special from you, Harley," he said as he closed the door behind him.

"You always do." Harley turned to face Jack. She hugged him, kissing him on the mouth. "I've missed you, Jack. You shouldn't stay away for so long."

Jack pulled away from Harley's embrace then started to unbutton his shirt.

Harley took one look at the bed, looked back at Jack and laughed. "Guess that's it for the foreplay—looks like someone's in a hurry."

twelve

Jack threw his cell phone into the trash can of their dressing room. Molly's voicemail was full, and she wasn't replying to any of his texts.

"Great shot there, Jackie boy, but I don't think you should throw out your phone for five points," Axl teased as he retrieved the undamaged cell phone and handed it back to his friend. "I wouldn't get so upset over a one-night stand. Believe me; there's another girl just like her waiting out there in the wings. All you have to do is give her the nod. It works for me."

"It's not like that. She's not like that," Jack said angrily. "If she'd just pick up the damned phone, I'd know what the problem is and fix it." He glanced at his cell phone's screen before pocketing it.

"Women," Ben muttered.

"You said it, Ben. Women. They're only good for one thing." Axl laughed. "No, make that three things."

"Leave me out of this," Matt said raising his hands. "You're a pig. You know that?"

"Maybe, but right now I'm the bassist in the world's hottest band, and I'm trying to get myself pumped for our show which is in less than ten minutes. It would be nice if our lead singer pulled his head out of his ass and got pumped, too. If not, I think we're only going to be playing sad love songs for two and a half hours."

"I'm not playing 'Molly's Rain' for two and a half hours," Ben yelled from across the room.

Jack had to admit it. Ben and Axl were right. His head had been up his ass for quite awhile. He'd been haunted by his dreams and missing Molly. All he could think about was her. He made it through last night's concert with the belief that Molly would talk to him. He still hadn't heard her voice. He couldn't let her get to him like this. He and the guys had made a pact—no letting personal shit interfere with the show. They had to give one hundred percent to the fans. They deserved that much.

"You're right, Ben. No 'Molly's Rain' tonight. It's off our playlist until I get things sorted out with her. If it's over, the song is gone, too."

"Hey, it's a good song," Matt offered. "Dump it from the playlist for now, but we're recording it when this tour is over."

"That's right," Ben agreed.

"Five minutes," someone yelled at them from the hallway.

"Let's give them a show they won't forget," Jack said.

"Dragon Slayers!" the foursome shouted as they pumped their fists.

XO XO XO

"Stop staring at your cell phone. Either call him or block his number."

Molly turned off her phone and pocketed it in her jeans back pocket. Her cell phone buzzed all day alerting her to voice messages and texts. They were all from Jack.

"I didn't think it would be this hard. I miss him, Jess."

"You knew the guy for one night. How special could he possibly be?"

"We had this connection." Molly picked up a soft towel and started polishing the glassware.

"Right, and now the thought of seeing him again scares the hell out of you. Not the right kind of connection, in my opinion."

"Not fair! Jack's an amazing guy. He's drop dead gorgeous, great in bed, and he likes me."

"Amazing? Maybe. Gorgeous. Yes. Great in bed? Beginner's luck more like it, and you haven't had sex with a man in months so that bad sex would have been great for you."

"I hate you." Molly swatted Jess with her towel.

"You'll get over Jack. Give it time, sweetie. Trust me. You're doing the right thing."

XO XO XO

Their concert rocked—four encores before management turned on the house lights. The roadies were threatening to quit if the band didn't stop playing. There wouldn't be enough time to dismantle their stage, load the trucks and get to Portland in time for the next concert.

Jack stumbled onto the tour bus. Exhaustion hit him hard once the adrenalin rush from performing left his body. He tried to keep up with the guys, drinking and flirting with the female fans. He hugged and kissed more girls than he cared to remember. Falling into his bed, Jack closed his eyes and passed out within seconds.

Molly came to him in his dreams. He knew the shape of her face, the curve of her lips and her blue-grey eyes that sparkled as she gave him her sinfully sexy smile. Her lips were full and luscious, her kiss hot and delicious, and her breath sweet when she kissed him. He missed her. It had only been a few days since she had last visited him in his dreams. Jack was afraid that she had abandoned him and found another man to love, another man to torture in his sleep.

"You've been a bad boy, Jack Thomas."

The soft purr of her voice in his ear made his cock jerk to attention.

"What did I do wrong? Why won't you return my calls?"

"You know why."

"No, I don't." He reached out for her. She slipped away from his hands, laughing at his fumbling. "Please don't go."

"Why did you let her touch you? Why did you let her make her mark on you?"

"Who?"

"You know who. Don't lie to me, Jack."

Jack reached out for Molly again. "Please let me hold you. Let me know that you still want me."

"It's not that easy," she said as she turned away from him.

"Let me fix it. You have to let me fix it. My heart's breaking. Let me love you again. Please."

"Do you think we can kiss and make it better?" Suddenly she was face to face with him, her sweet breath on his face, her mouth close to his. Her lips parted as her tongue darted out and licked his bottom lip.

"Yes," he moaned as he took her in his arms and kissed her.

"Kiss me harder," she whispered against his lips.

He pulled her in tight, kissing her as though his life depended on it. As long as he held her and loved her, she'd forgive him. She had to.

Jack awoke to the ringing of his cell phone. He reached automatically into his front pants pocket and pulled out the irritating device.

"Hello," he managed to croak.

"Jack, it's Dad. We haven't heard from you in a few days. Your mother asked me to give you a call. She wants to know how things are going with your ladylove."

Jack looked at his dual time wristwatch, forcing his sleepy eyes to focus. "Dad, it's five o'clock in the morning."

"Your point being?"

"I've been asleep for three hours. Tell Mom I'll call her later."

Jack ended the call and dropped his phone on the bed. Burying his head into his pillow, he tried to fall back to sleep. Images from his dream haunted him. Molly was mad at him. What was it? *She marked you.* Who marked him? Did Molly know about the after party? Were pictures posted on the internet? Did he do something he couldn't remember?

"Fuck this."

Jack sat up in his bunk, hitting his head on the overhead light. He cursed again, pressing the palm of his hand against the top of his head. It was then that he noticed he was dressed in his clothes from last night, boots, too. Jack pulled off his boots then climbed out of his bunk. He made his way to the bathroom, stripping off his clothes as he walked.

He stood in the shower, his arms outstretched, palms pressed against the tiles, as cold water sprayed over him. Jack didn't mind the cold water. He'd become used to cold showers since Molly haunted his dreams.

The words *she marked you* played in his brain like an earworm. Jack believed in the power of dreams, something he learned from stories his parents told him. Molly was telling him something, the reason why she couldn't be with him. *She marked you.* No one marked him. He'd never been with a woman, except for Molly. She left a mark on his heart the moment he sat down and gazed into her eyes. *She marked me.*

Jack's gaze fell to his left forearm. The redness had left where Harley had touched up his tattoo. She marked him. With red and black ink, she gave Molly's name a permanent place on his arm. It couldn't be this one tattoo. Molly hadn't seen it. She hadn't seen any of his tattoos, any of his marks.

"Damn it." The realization hit Jack hard. Molly wasn't returning his calls because of his tattoos. She'd made the decision that she couldn't see him. She didn't want to be with him, give him the chance to convince her that they could be together.

Jack finished his shower and dressed quickly into jeans and a T-shirt. He made his way to the front of the bus. He stopped in the galley to take a carton of chocolate milk from the fridge, and then made his way to the lounge area.

"Good morning," the driver greeted him, keeping his eyes on the road. "Just five more hours until we arrive in Portland."

"Good morning," Jack said as he noticed the windshield wipers moving slowly back and forth over the windshield.

Jack sat on the couch and gazed out of the window. Rain. Molly. He couldn't separate the two. He couldn't look at rain without thinking of her, her smile and her optimism that good things happened after a rainstorm. He couldn't think of Molly without thinking of the dark cloud that hovered over her, her father's death and her fear of tattoos. If only she could look at him, really look at him, she'd know that she had nothing to fear. He had to make things right with Molly. He had to convince her that they could be together. Jack pulled out his cell phone from his pants pocket and pressed speed dial.

"Hey, Jackie, I hear your father woke you up earlier. I'm sorry about that. I had nothing to do with him making the call." His mother never said hello when she saw his name appear on her phone. She always spoke to him as though he were in the room with her. No hellos or goodbyes. Davina didn't like goodbyes.

"It's okay, Mom. How are you?"

"Today's a great day! I'm talking with you and Stevie sent me a wonderful email with pictures of Budapest. David sent me a good morning text."

"How's my little brother?"

"Busy with exams. Oh, everyone is coming out for Mother's Day. Will you be here? I'd love it if you could come."

"Wouldn't miss it for the world." Jack took a drink from the milk carton. "Mom?"

"Yes, Jackie?"

"How did Dad convince you to love him?"

Jack smiled at the sound of his mother's soft laugh. He could imagine the sparkle in her eyes as she recalled the occasion.

"Your father has the gift of persuasion. He constantly talked about how we were meant to be lovers and that it was fate that brought us together. He pleaded with me to see things his way. He wouldn't stop."

"Was he annoying?"

"No, I wouldn't say that. Your father was determined, stubborn and sure of himself. He didn't have a Plan B. I had to love him. He said there was no other choice."

There was a brief silence between them. "Jackie? What's wrong?"

"My tattoos terrify her. Something from her past—she witnessed her father's murder and the guy who did it had tattoos."

"Oh my. That's awful!"

"We were fine until she saw me."

"Your ink is a lot to take in, dear, even if a person isn't afraid of tattoos."

"You got over it."

"Not quite, Jack. Every once in awhile, I feel my heart stop when I see that monster on your back."

"I didn't know that. You never told me."

"That's because I love you. I understand the reason behind your tattoos. It's just that sometimes it's hard to see my baby's beautiful skin coloured in."

"How do I get her to look at me and not be afraid, Mom? How did you do it?"

"Jackie, I've always loved you. What's the saying? Love is colour blind. You are beautiful on the inside and the outside. I've never stopped thinking that."

"So, what do I do?"

"Show her who you are inside. Get her to know the man underneath the ink. Tell her your story. Read it to her. Sing it to her. If you can do that, she may come to accept your tattoos."

"Tell her my story," Jack repeated the words, realizing that he'd overlooked the most obvious solution. "Mom, I love you."

"Me, too, Jackie. Good luck and make sure I see you on Mother's Day."

The call ended. Jack placed his cell phone on the table. His mom was right. He had to tell Molly his story. He listened to hers, and now it was time for her to give him the chance to tell his.

thirteen

"Why are you listening to his music?"

Molly looked up from her laptop screen. "I may not be able to look at the guy, but his music is really good. You even think so."

Jess flopped onto the leather couch and put her feet up on the battered coffee table. She picked up the stuffed dragon, a new addition to Molly's leather couch, and hugged it. She wished she could hug Molly and make everything right with her.

Jess gave out a heavy sigh. "It's dead out there tonight. We have to bring in some entertainment and get this place rocking. There's a new bar slated to open in a couple of months. We need to make sure we keep the college students coming here. Get a strong customer base before they're tempted to try out the competition."

"Last time we brought in a guitarist it didn't work out very well, remember?"

"If you hadn't slept with him, it may have."

"He could only play five songs, Jess."

"Oh, right. He sucked, didn't he?"

"More than you know." Molly groaned as she raised her arms above her head and stretched. "Okay, you find the entertainment this time and make sure it's no one you'd sleep with, and I'll stay clear of him."

"What if it's a female guitarist?"

"She's all yours."

Jess stuck her tongue out at Molly. "Gee, thanks. So, have you given this cutie a name?" she asked, holding up the large stuffed dragon and shaking it gently at Molly.

"No."

"What about Finley?"

"Finley the Dragon?"

"Yep. I think it's a cute name for a dragon."

"I'll think about it." Molly turned her attention to her computer screen.

"The flowers Jack sent you still look great. He must have spent a fortune on them. Not that money is a problem for him."

"I guess not," Molly muttered.

"Where did you put the box of chocolates he sent you? I was hoping to try the chocolate covered almonds. They're my favourite."

"None left."

"You ate them all? Molly, you little pig. That was five pounds of chocolate you scarfed down in a day."

"I was hungry. Besides, he sent them to me. I didn't see your name on the card."

"I wonder what Jack will send you tomorrow. I hope it's a car, one of those expensive sports cars that go from zero to one hundred in a nanosecond. Oh, and it has to be red. Cherry red with Italian black leather interior and a kick-ass sound system."

"I'm trying to work here. We have orders to send in. You know, because we run a bar and a restaurant."

"You've already done that. I checked. What are you looking at?"

Jess knew Molly better than she knew her own sister. She knew every mood swing, every silly habit, and every secret of her best friend and boss. She also knew when her friend was in pain. Molly tried to conceal the dark circles under her eyes, but there was no hiding the dullness in her eyes. She'd lost her sparkle, and it ate at Jess knowing that it was because of a guy.

Molly had bad breakups before. However, they were nothing compared to this. Usually, all it took was a night of partying and the ex-boyfriend was soon forgotten. This time was different. Molly wasn't partying, and she most certainly hadn't forgotten Jack. Not that he was letting her.

Every day a package arrived for Molly with a note that read, *You belong in my story.*

"I Googled Jack. I want to know more about him."

"You want to know more about the guy you dumped?"

"Yes."

"So, you can be bought," Jess mused. "Don't tell me his presents are making you change your mind. Molly, you can't be serious."

"I haven't changed my mind, and no, he can't buy me with presents. I'm trying to find out why he got all those tattoos. Why would someone, as drop dead gorgeous as he is, mark himself like that? Tattoos are for-ever. I just don't get it."

"That's what some people do. They get one and then it leads to another. Soon the person is covered with them, and there isn't one bit of untouched skin left on the entire body." Jess stood up and headed to the office door, still carrying the stuffed dragon. "Here's an idea. Why don't you ask him?"

Molly looked over at Jess with amazement.

"You never thought of that, did you?"

She tossed the dragon at Molly and then shook her head as she closed the door behind her.

XO XO XO

"Maguire's. Jess speaking."

"Hi, Jess. It's Jack Thomas."

"Hold on." Jess took a quick look around to make sure Molly wasn't within earshot. "Why are you calling?"

"I think you know why. Is something wrong with Molly? Why hasn't she returned my calls?"

"Jack." Jess stopped to think about her answer. Was it her place to speak for Molly? She'd tried to get Molly to send at least one message to Jack, at least to thank him for her presents; however, Molly refused.

"Can you talk?"

"Yes, I can talk."

"It's because of my tattoos, isn't it? I need to know, Jess."

Jess took one more look for Molly before she spoke. "Her nightmares are back. They haven't been this bad since I've known her."

"What kind of nightmares? You mean the ghosts?"

"Yes, except it's not the usual ghosts scaring the hell out of her anymore."

"What do you mean by that?"

Jess closed her eyes, wishing she was anywhere but here. She liked Jack. He just wasn't the right man for Molly.

Jack's impatience got the better of him as he barked into the phone, "Tell me now, Jess."

"It's you, Jack. Her nightmares are about you. You're the monster that's haunting her."

Jack slumped against his seat as though she'd punched him in the stomach.

"She stayed up one night watching your music videos. Molly thought that if she forced herself to see your tattoos, she'd be able to see them for real. Her plan backfired, and she ended up scaring herself shitless. I'm sorry, Jack, but she's a wreck where you're concerned."

"I would never hurt her."

"I know that, and I know she does, too. You have to realize that her nightmares are too real for her. They stay with her long after she's awake. It takes a lot of coffee to get her settled in the morning."

"I have to make things right with her. I can't leave her like this."

"There's nothing you can do. Trust me."

"I can't just walk away. I did this to her."

There was a long silence over the phone. Only the background music from the bar let Jack know that Jess was still on the line.

"When's your tour over?"

"We're done for now. Axl came down with mono, so we've had to cancel the last leg of our tour. Why do you ask?"

Jess chewed on her bottom lip as she wrestled with getting involved in Molly's love life. She'd already told Jack too much. Molly could hate her for what she was about to tell Jack. "Have you ever played in a bar?"

"Molly offered me a job before she knew who I was. Are you offering me a gig?"

"We agreed to bring in a guitar player and Molly gave me full control over who gets hired. There's a job here if you want it. Minimum wage plus tips. How does that sound?"

"When do I start?"

fourteen

He caught Jess's attention the moment he entered Maguire's. Wearing faded denim jeans and a long-sleeved blue shirt tucked in at the waist, the man was perfection on two legs. There was no other way to describe him. Handsome didn't quite cut it, and good looking was too generic. If only he didn't have those blasted tattoos, Jess wouldn't have to get involved in helping him change Molly's mind. She knew Molly would pull a hissy fit the minute she saw Jack, and she didn't care. Her friend was a wreck, and Jack was the only person who could help her. Jess hoped and prayed that she wasn't making a huge mistake.

Jack stopped just inside the door and looked around him, searching for Molly. It had been too long since he'd seen the woman who had captured his heart and taken his virginity. He wondered if she knew how special that moment was to him.

Jess walked around the bar toward him. She opened the door and looked outside to the curb. Her frown showed her disappointment. "Nope."

"What's the nope for?"

"No cherry red sports car with Italian black leather seats."

Jack fished car keys out of his front jeans pocket and handed them to Jess. "What about this. Will this do?"

Jess pressed the panic button on the key fob. The honking of the horn brought her attention to a shiny black Volkswagen Beetle convertible. She ran to the car and caressed the exterior as she walked around the car, taking in every detail.

"She belonged to my dad," Jack said proudly from the curb. "I know she's old, but she still drives like a dream."

"Stick shift?"

"Of course. I've added GPS and upgraded the stereo. The old one died. Other than that, she's the real deal, still in mint condition." Jack waited while Jess finished appraising his car. "Does she pass?"

"Yes, she does. A woman can tell a lot about a man from the car he drives."

"What does this car tell you about me?"

"That Molly's got a keeper, Jack. A real keeper." She hooked her arm through his and started toward the door. "Come on, let's get you settled in."

"Where's Molly?"

"She's out running errands. She knows that the entertainment starts tonight, but not that you're it."

Jack stopped. "What?"

"Don't worry," she said tugging on his arm. "She'll be thrilled to see you. She just doesn't know it yet."

When they reached the bar, Jack leaned his guitar case against it and took a seat on a barstool while Jess tended the bar. She filled two glasses with draft beer and offered one to Jack.

"There's a tiny stage over in that corner," she said while pointing to it. "We've got a sound system that's pretty good. Let me know what else you need, and I'll try to have it for you for tonight."

Jack looked over at the stage. "Looks good from here. All I need is a stool."

"No problem. I'll get you one. Cheers," Jess said as she touched her glass to his.

"Cheers." Jack shifted in his seat. "How is she today?"

"If I didn't know better, I'd swear she's come down with something. She's so pale and tired looking. She won't talk about the nightmares anymore. She thinks that if she ignores them, they'll go away."

"I have to make this right, Jess."

"We both do, Jack. We both do."

XO XO XO

Driving back to Maguire's, after completing what felt like an endless to-do list supplied by Jess, Molly noticed heavy traffic along the main drag. Traffic moved at a crawl, and every curbside parking space was filled—not the usual Wednesday night in Ingledale. When she finally made it to Maguire's, there was a line up to get into the bar. Something was up, and she was sure Jess was behind it.

Molly drove her van around the corner and entered the back parking lot. She was relieved to find that no one had dared park in her reserved parking space. She took what she could carry out of the van, locked it and then made her way to the employee entrance.

Once inside, Molly stopped when she heard him. She'd listened to one too many of his songs never to forget his voice. Even without the backup of his band, there was no mistaking the sweet tenor sound of Jack Thomas. She waited until he finished, somehow feeling that it would be rude to walk to the kitchen while he sang. Molly closed her eyes and let every word flow over her. She remembered this feeling, the way she felt when he didn't take his eyes off her, singing only to her. Molly dropped her packages, letting them fall to the floor. Her right hand rubbed at the pain in her chest, knowing that he still had that hold on her.

Molly heard the applause followed by Jack thanking the patrons. He told them he was taking a fifteen-minute break. Molly gathered up her packages and took refuge in her office without letting Jess know she had returned.

Jack saw that the office light was on. He knew that Molly was back. He could feel it. The ache in his heart let him know that she was near. He tapped lightly on the door and then opened it without waiting for an invitation.

"Jack," Molly said from her desk, her gaze fixed on her laptop screen.

"Molly," he answered in a low voice that made her toes curl.

"So, you're our guitarist."

"I had time on my hands, and you had made the offer for me to play here remember?"

"That was before I knew who you were."

"Nothing's changed," he said with a shrug. "I play the guitar. You need someone to draw in the customers. It looks by the crowd out there that it's a good night for business." Jack made his way to her desk. "Molly, we both know you're not reading anything on that screen. Look at me and let's talk."

She looked up at him with teary eyes. "I can't. I just can't."

In seconds, Jack was around the desk. Grabbing Molly, he pulled her up from her chair and took her in his arms. He kissed her hard. Too many days and nights without the sound of her voice, missing her touch, vanished with one kiss.

"No more can't. No more won't. No more don't. We're going to get through this. Let me help you. I started it. Let me finish it. Let me rid you of those nightmares once and for all."

"It's not that simple."

"It is. Trust me."

"What are you, my knight in shining armour?"

There it was again, the mischievous smile that could make her believe in anything. "Yes. I'm your knight in shining armour. I'm your dragon slayer. There's no stopping me when I have my ladylove to rescue." Jack kissed the top of her head. "Don't shut me out, Molly. Please don't shut me out again. My heart is aching for you."

"The nightmares. They're about you."

"I know. Jess told me. I'm sorry."

"They seem so real."

"I'm real, too. Let me help you."

Molly relaxed in his arms. She wanted desperately to believe in him. Her heart ached to believe him.

"Trust me," he said, as though hearing her thoughts. "Trust me to show you that I'm no monster."

"I know you're not a monster."

"Then we're halfway there."

Jess opened the door and stopped when she saw Molly in Jack's arms. "Hey! No sleeping with the guitarist. You promised!"

Jack gazed down at Molly, his eyes sparkling. "Do you always sleep with the guitarist?"

Molly's cheeks heated from embarrassment. She buried her face in his shirt.

"I don't mind," he chuckled. "As long as I'm that guy."

XO XO XO

Molly locked the doors and turned off the neon OPEN sign. Maguire's had enjoyed one of its busiest nights on record. All thanks to the gorgeous and talented guitarist who was now sitting at her bar enjoying a glass of chocolate milk and a burger. She made her way back to the bar and took the seat next to Jack.

"Thank you."

He turned to look at her and smiled. "You're welcome. I enjoyed myself."

"How did people know you were playing tonight?" She looked at Jack and then at Jess.

"I couldn't advertise it in print, or else you'd know," Jess explained. "All it took was a couple of tweets that a certain lead singer of a certain band would be here, and then they were lined up at the door."

"The wonders of social media," Jack mused.

"What's the plan?"

"What do you mean?"

"How long are you planning to play here? Is it just tonight or are you staying for awhile? If we're going to be busy like this every night, we'll have to make some changes. We'll have to order more food, schedule more staff—"

"I'm here for a few weeks if you want me. Axl has mono and has to rest, Matt's off on holiday with his girlfriend, and Ben's at home working on some new songs. If you don't want my guitar talents, fine, but I'm staying until we get your nightmares dealt with, alright?"

"You're staying," Jess said with authority. "I love it when this place is rocking. Molly needs you, too. So, it's settled."

"And on that note, it's time for me to say good night. I've had a long day, and there is a king-sized bed waiting for me." Jack stood and zipped up his leather jacket.

"You're staying in a hotel?"

"Molly, it's for the best, at least for tonight until we have a chance to talk."

"You're probably right. Come here for breakfast. I can make it for you. We can start our talk then."

"Looking forward to it." He leaned down and kissed her on her forehead. "Good night, love. See you tomorrow. Good night, Jess."

XO XO XO

Loud banging roused Jack from a deep sleep. It took him a moment to get his bearings and find the bedside light. He stumbled to the door, wearing only his boxer briefs, and opened it to find Molly visibly upset.

"Make them go away," she said as she fell into his arms.

"Oh, Molly," he moaned, feeling her pain and fear. "Tell me what you need, and I'll do it."

"Hold me. Hold me until I fall asleep. Please."

Jack closed the door and led Molly to his bed. He helped her with her coat, surprised to find her naked underneath. She turned off the lights and scrambled under the covers.

"I need to put something on," Jack said as he fumbled with his suitcase.

"No. I want to feel your skin against mine. No shirt, Jack."

"I can't. If you wake up and see me, you could freak out. I can't be responsible for that."

"No saying can't, Jack. Your rules, remember?"

"Not where this is concerned. I won't risk it."

Jack pulled a long-sleeved T-shirt out of his suitcase and put it on. Once dressed, he crawled into bed beside Molly, who snuggled into his chest instantly.

"Hold me, Jack. Let me fall asleep in your arms. Keep the nightmares away."

Jack lay on his side and watched Molly sleep. He'd never had an angel in his bed before, and Molly was damned close to being that angel. Her blonde hair framed her face on the oversized pillow. Luscious pink lips formed the cutest pout. He longed to lean over and kiss her, only resisting because he didn't want to disturb this perfect moment. Molly stretched and groaned a weak complaint against the morning.

"Good morning, angel," Jack sang to her with a velvet voice warm and inviting.

She opened her eyes slowly, searching for the source of the voice she loved. "Hey."

"Hey, yourself. How are you?"

"Better. Thanks for letting me sleep with you."

"The pleasure is all mine." He leaned toward her and kissed her forehead. "Do you mind if I ask you something?"

"No. Go ahead."

"Do you sleep in the nude or are you only naked when you come to visit me?"

Molly laughed. "I sleep in the nude. I was in such a rush to get to you that I didn't dress. Does that bother you?"

"Not in the least. I'm a rock star. Naked women show up at my door all of the time. I'm quite used to it." He kissed her again. "You are the only woman I've let past the door."

"Why is that?"

"You know why."

"No, I don't. Not really. Why did you wait for me before you had sex? It's not like it's a big taboo to have sex before marriage, not that we're getting married."

"I didn't want to. I had always dreamed of how it would be for me when I met that certain someone." He kissed her on the nose and smiled. "And I knew when I met you that you were the one."

"I've been with other men. Didn't you want to have a virgin?"

"That wasn't a priority of mine."

"Why not?" She traced her finger over his shirt, gradually making her way down to the waistband of his boxers.

Jack sighed heavily. He turned from her and got out of bed.

"Jack?"

"We have to talk first, and it's going to be hard enough without you lying naked beside me."

"I thought you did tell me your story. You waited for me. You got me. The end." She smiled at him, tempting him with her pale blue-grey eyes with a sparkle that was absent last night. Molly pulled down the covers, exposing her nakedness to him.

Jack ogled her for the longest time, taking in every delicate and gorgeous inch of her body. He wanted her, but he wouldn't jeopardize this morning, not now when there was too much to lose. "We're not having sex." Jack opened the closet door and pulled out the hotel's complimentary bathrobe. He handed it to Molly. "Put this on, please. It's not fair that only one of us is wearing clothes."

Molly took the offering and put it on. "Now what?"

"How about I order room service, and we stay in for the morning? We can talk."

"I was supposed to make you breakfast."

"I'll take a rain check. Talking comes first."

"Fine. You order, and I'll take a shower. How's that?"

While Molly took her shower, Jack ordered breakfast and readied himself for telling his story. It would be a long morning, and he hoped she was willing to listen.

"Jack, you ordered enough for six people."

Jack shrugged. "I like my breakfast. Consider this a typical farm breakfast."

Molly filled her plate with eggs and sausage and a couple of blueberry pancakes. Jack went all out when he ordered room service. When she saw two carafes of coffee, she realized he meant business when he said they had to talk.

"This feels more like an intervention than storytelling."

"It is an intervention in a way. I'm trying to save you from your nightmares."

"You can't save me from them. I've had them since my father died."

"I can try to make you not see me in them. How's that?"

"Better." Molly rested her fork on her plate. "It's not your fault, you know. I did it to myself. I thought I could watch those videos of you, and I failed. By the way, why does every music video of yours have you half-naked with a woman who might as well be naked by the way she's dressed? What is it with all the skin?"

"Marketing, pure and simple. Me without a shirt sells more than me with a shirt."

"You took a survey?"

"I majored in music and business, Molly. I know."

"Geez. You'd think the sound of your voice would do all the selling. Your voice is incredible."

He smiled at her. "Thank you. As long as you like it, that's all that matters."

"Don't patronize me," she warned.

"I'm not. What I meant was that the only person that matters to me most is you. As long as you like my voice, no one else's opinion matters."

"Really?"

"Really."

"What if I can look at your tattoos and I hate them? What would you do?"

"You won't hate them."

"How can you say that?"

"Because I know that once you can look at them and know the story behind them, you will accept them. You don't have to love them. You only have to love me." He saw the doubt on her face. "It's all about trust, remember? I trust in your feelings for me that you'll accept them."

"You're pretty sure of yourself."

"I have to be. There's no other plan where you and I are concerned."

"So, you've got this all worked out, huh? You know how to change my mind?"

"No, I don't have this all worked out, but I promised myself that I would do my damnedest to make it right with you. I only want you, Molly Maguire, and I hope you want me enough to let me help you. Do you want me enough to let me try?"

Molly nodded her agreement, afraid that if she spoke, she'd start to cry, and she didn't want to cry. She'd done enough of that every night when her nightmares scared her awake.

Molly placed her empty plate on the coffee table. She watched with interest as Jack refilled his plate with pancakes. "I've never seen anyone eat that many pancakes before. You must love them."

"It's a family tradition. When we were little, Dad would make us pancakes for breakfast all of the time."

"Is he a part of your story, Jack?"

"Everyone in my life is a part of my story, Molly. Just like everyone in your life is a part of yours."

"I meant your tattoos. Is it because of your dad that you have your tattoos?"

"Yes and no." Jack put his empty plate on top of Molly's and stood up. "I have something to show you that will help you understand."

Jack walked over to his suitcase and pulled out two books, one an old leather journal, the other a children's storybook. He sat beside Molly and opened the leather book.

"My mother wrote these stories for my dad. It was her wedding present for him. She didn't have the chance to give it to him, her friend Maggie did, but that's another story."

"How many stories do you have?"

"A lifetime's worth. Mom wrote short stories for my dad in which he was the hero in every story. He was the dark knight who rode off on adventures, and she was his one true love. In every story, the dark knight rescues his ladylove from something or someone. One of the main baddies is a dragon."

"So, you are the son of a dragon slayer," Molly mused.

"You're smart," he smiled. "May I continue?"

She nodded her consent.

"When we were little, Dad told us these stories during playtime. It was always the knight, his ladylove, and a dragon. Stevie and I would add to the story and change it around, but the ending was always the same. The knight always returned to his true love, and they lived happily ever after."

"Did the dragon look like the one you sent me?"

"Yes. Do you like him?"

"His name is Finley."

Jack nodded his head and smiled. "Cool. That's a good name for a dragon. What about its mate? She should have a name."

"How does Fiona sound?"

"Finley and Fiona. I like it."

"So, what happened next?"

"We enjoyed the stories so much that Mom decided to write a children's version of them." Jack reached for the children's book. "Mom wrote this."

Molly took it from him; her eyes opened wide in surprise. "*Jack and Stevie's Bedtime Stories.* I remember this. Your mom wrote it? I thought she only wrote romance."

"Aren't fairy tales romance?" Jack snatched the book from her. "We will read this together. Later."

"Really?"

"Yes. Let me continue. It's important for you to know that these stories were a very important part of our lives. We lived a very normal life. We lived on a farm; we had chores; we went to public school—there was no Hollywood in our lives. Mom was just Mom. Dad was just Dad. We grew up in a very loving home with two parents who were deeply in love and showed us that love every day. We didn't know they were famous until we were ten years of age or older. That's how normal our lives were."

"No domestic servants?"

"None. We had to clean up after ourselves."

"No chauffeurs and limousines?"

"Only when necessary. We had bodyguards too, but we didn't know that. They fit in so well with our family when we traveled that I thought they were family."

"You had bodyguards?"

"Mom and Dad were super careful with us. There were some incidents."

"What?"

"Another story for another time."

"Fine," Molly relented. "What was it like when you found out who your parents were—I mean are?"

"Nothing changed. Not really. Do you remember the kid's movie, *Basset Hound Adventures*?"

"It was one of my favourites. I begged my mom for a basset hound puppy for months afterward. What about it?"

"Dad was the detective."

"Oh my gosh, he was, wasn't he?"

"Yes, and we didn't find out until we went to the premiere with him and Mom. We were all dressed up, and we drove to the theater in a limo. There were people all around us, calling out to my dad and taking pictures of us. We had no idea what was going on."

"He never told you?"

"No. Imagine our surprise when the movie started, and all of a sudden, Stevie and I realized our dad was on the screen. We looked at Mom, and she was watching our reaction, not the movie. Her smile told us everything we needed to know. Then we looked over at our little brother, David, and he pointed at the screen and yelled out, 'Daddy' and then he sat on Dad's lap for the rest of the movie, never making a sound. That's how we found out that Dad was Quinn Thomas, the actor."

"Wow."

"Yes, it was a wow moment."

"Do you ever watch his movies?"

"Once we were old enough, we watched his movies."

Jack took Molly's hand in his, seeing that she was derailing his story with her questions. "The point that I'm trying to make here is this. My parents' stories—their very own love story and the stories they told us, made me believe in the magic of love. I dreamed of finding and rescuing my true love. I dreamed of fighting dragons to save her, and I dreamed that one day I would find her, that I would find you."

Molly's face turned ashen as she hugged her abdomen.

"Molly, what's wrong?"

"I don't feel well. I think I'm going to be sick."

She jumped to her feet and ran to the bathroom, slamming the door behind her. Jack followed in quick pursuit. From behind the door, he could hear violent retching.

"Molly?"

"I'm okay."

Jack heard running water.

"I need something to wear. I've thrown up on my robe."

Jack retrieved a T-shirt from his suitcase and a pair of boxer briefs and returned to the bathroom door. "These should fit you."

Molly opened the door and took the offered clothes. When she finished cleaning up, she opened the door and exited the bathroom slowly.

"Are you okay?"

"I think I have the flu. I need to go home."

"No. Use my bed. I'll look after you."

"I really should go home. You don't need to see me like this."

Jack took her hand and led her to his bed. "Stay. I've got nowhere I have to be, and you need to sleep. Let me look after you."

Molly obeyed him. The velvety tone of his voice and the mesmerizing gaze of his eyes were a hard combination to resist. She got into bed and let him tuck her in under the warmth of the duvet.

"Jess. I have to call her. She'll be wondering where I am."

"I'll call her. You close your eyes. Try to rest."

"What about your story?"

"It can wait. Sleep."

Jack sat on the edge of the bed and sang to her. Molly didn't recognize the language, but the sound of his words and the sweet melody were hypnotic. She felt herself drifting off into sleep.

Jack left Molly's side to call Jess. He closed the bathroom door so as not to disturb her.

"Maguire's. Jess speaking."

"Hi, Jess. It's Jack. Molly's with me."

"I thought so when I didn't find her in her bed. How is she?"

"Sleeping right now. She's come down with the stomach flu."

"It figures. She hasn't been sleeping. Her body must be worn out."

"That's what I'm thinking, too. She'll stay here and rest. I'll come in around the same time tonight."

"Thanks, Jack. I appreciate you looking after her."

"There's no need to thank me."

Jack ended the call. He showered and dressed in jeans and a long-sleeved shirt. He rolled up the sleeves just enough so that he could see Molly's name on his left wrist. He kissed her name and then watched over his sleeping angel.

XO XO XO

She found him stretched out on the couch fast asleep. His right arm covered his eyes, and his left arm hung over the edge of the couch. Even in sleep, Jack was gorgeous. From his perfect bare toes all the way up to the top of his head, there was nothing about him she'd change. Molly noticed that his right forearm was free of tattoos a couple of inches above his wrist. She glanced down at his left arm to see black and red ink. She looked away quickly.

"You can do this," she whispered. "It's just a little bit of ink. It doesn't look like a monster."

Molly closed her eyes and took a deep breath. Two inches. That's all it was. Surely, she could look at two inches of ink and not freak out. She blew out. She looked back at Jack's left arm. She wondered how such a loving man could have monsters inked on his body. Why would he ruin perfection? She knelt on the floor and touched his wrist. Instinctively her eyes closed, protecting herself. She forced them open and stared at the ink until her eyes focused.

It was a rose. A red rose outlined in black, and in that rose was her name. She looked up at Jack's face. How could he be so sure that she'd be his lover? What made him put her name on his body forever? Molly reached out tentatively and touched her name. She traced the delicate letters, awed by the beauty of the design that created her name. He loved her. After knowing her for a day, this man loved her.

"Molly?" Jack asked, still half asleep.

She scrambled on top of him and buried her face into his chest. Jack embraced her and kissed the top of her head.

"You have my name on your wrist."

"Yes, I do."

"I never thought that a tattoo could look so beautiful."

Unwilling to ruin the moment with words, Jack hummed.

"That's my song."

Jack continued to hum.

Molly recited the lyrics, "And I love her more than words can say, more than ink can show. I'll love my Molly every day, and with each day, my love will grow."

"Always," he vowed.

"Don't give up on us, Jack. Fight for me."

fifteen

"So? How is she?" Jess asked from behind the bar.

Jack took a seat and accepted the offered draft beer.

"She's feeling better." He took a long drink from his glass.

"Looks like you needed that. What happened between you two?"

"We talked. We haven't finished, but we're getting there."

He looked up at Jess with a sparkle in his eyes. "She saw this." He pulled up his sleeve to show her his tattoo. "I know it's not much, but—"

"It's freaking amazing," Jess finished for him. "I don't believe it. Did she look at just that or your whole arm?"

"We didn't force it. Molly saw this and touched it. She loves it."

"Well, I guess so. She has her name tattooed on one of the hottest rock stars alive."

"I don't think she cares about that."

"You're right. She doesn't. But it is pretty cool knowing that a guy would do that for you."

"I didn't do it for her." There was no ignoring Jess's arched eyebrow and the slight tilt of her head. "Okay, maybe a small part of me did it for her. She's part of my story. Molly's name belongs there. It always has."

XO XO XO

When Jack returned to his hotel suite with an overnight bag filled with Molly's clothes and toiletries, he found Molly curled up in bed reading his mother's book.

"Hey there," she greeted him, looking up over the worn pages of the leather journal. "How's your new job as a bar singer going?"

"Great! Standing room only again. Jess was happy." Jack placed his guitar case and Molly's overnight bag on the floor. He took off his leather jacket and hung it on the back of a chair before making his way to Molly's bedside.

"How are you feeling? I thought you'd be sleeping," Jack asked as he sat down on the bed beside her.

"I couldn't put this book down. Jack, it's amazing. Your mom never published this?"

"No, it was written for my dad. That's the only copy that I know of."

"Why do you have it?"

"It's on loan. If I lose it or damage it, I'm dead."

"I can see why. This book is very personal reading. Does it embarrass you when you read this?"

"What do you mean?"

"Reading the sex scenes and seeing how much they love each other."

"No. Should it?"

"I know I wouldn't be able to look at my parents if I read about them having sex against a wall." Molly sighed. "The image of her calling out his name when he brings her to orgasm is so hot."

Jack took the book from her hands and placed it on the bedside table. "They're adults, and they have sex. I'm glad about that or else I wouldn't be here with you."

"But—"

"Just think of the love, Molly. That's what I learned to do." He leaned over and kissed her.

"What does that mean? Learned to do?"

Jack settled against the headboard. Molly cuddled into his side, and gazed up at him, waiting for him to speak.

"When I was thirteen, I had a falling out with my dad."

"What teenager doesn't?"

"Not many teenagers have to deal with their father's infidelity and an illegitimate brother."

"You mean his child with Rene Adams?"

Jack's hand caressed Molly's arm while he searched for the right words to tell her. "I remember when Dad brought David home. Stevie and I were four years old. We were thrilled to have a baby brother. We knew he was family, and nothing else mattered to us. My parents never hid the fact that Rene was David's birth mother and that my dad was his father."

"How did it become a problem for you?"

Jack smiled at Molly's directness. "When you're thirteen, going through puberty, and everyone in your school knows who you are and who your father is—that's how. Kids can be cruel and relentless. They would download shit about Dad, how he slept around, how he treated Mom, and then they would say things about David. Most of it wasn't true, and I knew it, but it sure hurt like hell."

"What did you do?"

"I took it out on Dad. I wouldn't look at him, and if he spoke to me, I ignored him or told him to fuck off. I hated him. I hated what he did to Mom. I hated that his fame was the cause of all the crap I was going through, and I ran away."

"For a long time?"

"No. My dad found me and instead of taking me home, he took me on a plane, and we ended up on a private island in the Caribbean. It was just the two of us in this beach house. No internet, no telephone, no TV. Dad told me we'd be staying there until he got through to me. It was my choice."

"How long did that take?"

"How long would you last without your cell phone, internet or TV?"

"That fast, huh?"

"Dad asked me to trust him that whatever he told me was the truth, and it was in complete confidence. Not even my mother knew some of what he was going to tell me."

"What did he tell you or is that a secret?"

"Dad told me about his relationship with Rene and the truth behind David's conception. We talked about Mom, and he said she was the love of his life, and he regretted hurting her. If it weren't for my mom, he didn't know if he'd have been strong enough to accept David as his son."

"Shit."

"That's not all of it. We talked about sex and the Hollywood scene, and how he managed being a celebrity. He told me about the women and the emptiness he felt. Dad wasn't proud of some of the things he'd done. It scared the hell out of him to know that he could lose me because of his past. He asked me to forgive him."

"And you did."

"Yes, I did. It took me awhile. I was a stubborn know-it-all teenager, remember?"

"What are you now?"

"I'm a stubborn know-it-all man."

Molly reached up and caressed his cheek. "Is your dad the reason why you stayed a virgin?"

"I don't know. I saw what he and Mom had, and I wanted that. I still do. I remember that I was terrified of getting a girl pregnant even though my parents made sure all of us knew about practicing safe sex. Instead of girls, I focused all of my energy on Dragon Slayers. I didn't want anything or anyone interfering with my dream."

"What about me, dragon slayer? Am I interfering with your dream?"

Molly reached for Jack and pulled him onto her. She kissed him and was eager for more.

Jack pulled away, taking her hands in his. "You are my dream, Molly. You've always been with me."

"Are we going to make love?"

"Not yet, sweetheart, we've got another story to read," Jack said as he slipped off the bed and headed to the bathroom.

"You're torturing me," Molly called out to him. "How am I supposed to get to know you better if you won't touch me?"

"I never said that I wouldn't touch you. We're not having sex that's all."

Molly scrambled out of the bed and followed Jack. She stood in the doorway and watched him turn on the shower.

He turned and faced her, his hands on the top button of his shirt. "Now is not the time. You don't want to see me undress."

"Yes, I do."

He smiled at her as he took a few steps toward her. "Let me rephrase then. You do want to see me undress, but you don't want to see what's underneath. Give us time, angel. Don't rush this."

Molly noticed the frosted glass of the shower's doors.

"May I watch you shower?"

"So, you like to watch men shower and sleep with guitarists." Jack nodded his approval. "You've got a kinky side to you."

"No, I don't. I want to see you naked and seeing you through that glass gives me the perfect opportunity to do so."

"Having a hard time picturing what's under these clothes?"

There it was, the mischievous smile tempting and teasing her all at once.

"I'm pretty sure of what's underneath," she murmured. "Just give me a peek."

"Promise me you'll walk out of the bathroom if you see more than you can manage." He saw a wicked grin form on her face. "I'm talking about my tattoos. If you can't manage seeing my tattoos."

"I promise."

Jack put down the toilet seat lid and motioned for her to sit. Molly took the offered seat and smiled.

"How's that for viewing?"

"Perfect."

"Close your eyes. I'll let you know when you can look."

Molly closed her eyes. She smiled in anticipation of seeing Jack naked, even if it would be through frosted glass. Anything was better than nothing, having seen only his face and the two inches of skin above his wrist. Molly's curiosity was getting the best of her, especially now that she'd read his mother's explicit stories.

Jack undid his belt buckle and pulled it from his jeans. He handed the soft leather strap to Molly. She took the belt and ran her hands over the large buckle. The metal was cool to the touch. She could feel a design in the buckle. Her finger traced the outline.

"That was handmade for me by a family friend for my seventeenth birthday. It's the only one I wear."

"It's a dragon," Molly said as she ran her fingers over the raised scales on the buckle. "What a surprise."

"Are you making fun of me?" Jack's mouth was on hers instantly. His kiss was hard and powerful.

"No," she answered, breathless once he released her.

"Good. Now keep your eyes closed and don't let go of that belt."

Jack took his time undoing the buttons on his fly. He made sure that Molly heard each button pop as it released from its buttonhole.

He focused on her mouth, how her lips parted slightly, allowing her tongue to lick the bottom lip as though anticipating the taste of what she would see.

"What are you thinking?"

"Five buttons. Your fly has five buttons."

"You look like you want to eat the buttons, love."

"Not the buttons, Jack, definitely not the buttons." She heard his jeans fall to the floor. "You're killing me."

"You're the one who asked to be here. Is it too much for you? Do you need to leave?"

"No. Please let me stay."

Jack stepped toward her and kissed her again. Molly reached for him.

"Hold on to my belt, love. Keep your hands on my belt."

"You've done this before," she protested against his lips. "There's no way a virgin could know how to do this."

"I'm not a virgin. You were with me when I lost my virginity. Remember? Or have you forgotten that night?"

"I need a reminder." Molly caressed the leather belt, loving the feel of the leather between her hands. "This can't be your first seduction."

"Am I seducing you, angel?"

"Yes. That's what it feels like."

"If you think I'm seducing you, it's all in your mind." Jack undid the top buttons of his shirt and pulled it over his head. He held the shirt to her face, letting her take in his scent.

"What do you smell?"

"You."

"Tell me more."

"I smell Maguire's and stale beer. I smell your cologne. I don't know what label it is. It's very nice."

"Describe nice."

"Musk, man and hot, mind-blowing sex."

"I don't wear cologne. That smell is all mine."

"Fuck me."

"No."

"Why are you torturing me?"

Jack leaned down to whisper in her ear, his breath hot against her skin. Molly longed to feel that breath on her body.

"I have dreamed about you for as long as I can remember. In every dream, you torture me with your soft touch and your sweet kisses. You promise me that I can touch you, and then you leave me waking with this incredible ache for you."

"So, this is your revenge?"

"Not revenge, sweetheart, my reward." Jack kissed her cheek. "I'm going to shower now. I'll tell you when you can look."

Jack stepped into the shower, already fogging from the cascading hot water. He wanted to make sure Molly couldn't see his tattoos through the frosted glass. He reached for the liquid soap and made a thick lather on his torso and arms. It didn't matter that he couldn't reach his back. She wouldn't see it as long as he exposed his side to her. Jack aimed the showerhead away from him letting the water run down the far wall of the shower.

"You can look now, Molly. Tell me what you see."

Molly opened her eyes. She could see the outline of his body behind the frosted glass, but no markings on his skin.

"You cheated," she called out. "No fair."

Molly stood and walked to the shower door. She pressed her face against the glass, hoping to see more than the profile of her lover.

"You're covered in lather. At least show me your ass."

Jack laughed and turned, pressing his buttocks to the glass. He knew she wouldn't be afraid. His tattoos stopped at his waist.

Molly bent down and kissed the glass in appreciation of the fine specimen in front of her. "Show me more."

Jack crossed his arms to cover his torso before he turned to face her. Molly's eyes opened wide. Although she had held it in her hands weeks ago, she had not given his penis the attention it deserved. She remembered the feel of it, how it stretched and filled her. She felt her cheeks redden as she remembered how expertly he brought her to orgasm with his powerful strokes.

"Impressive."

"I'm glad you think so. Have you seen enough?"

Molly saw the hint of colour on Jack's arms. A grey leafy vine wound up his left arm up to his shoulder.

"Show me my name."

Jack turned his left arm, exposing the inner arm to her. Molly traced her finger along the glass, following the pattern of the vine. Her name was on his wrist, the only rose on the vine.

"There's no one else."

"This arm is reserved for you and our kids."

Molly sank to the floor. Tears filled her eyes. She wiped them away with the back of her hand.

"Damn it. Molly, please don't cry."

He rinsed off the lather as quickly as he could, then opened the shower door and reached for the bathrobe hanging on the wall and put it on.

Jack knelt beside her. "I'm sorry."

"For what?"

"For making you cry."

"Don't be. These are happy tears."

"Why?"

"Because you are so sure of us having a life together."

"There's no Plan B."

"What?"

"Never mind. We'll get through this. I promise you. Come on, its time for bed."

Molly waited for Jack while he dressed in the bathroom. He was so sure of them having a life together that it made her heart ache. Was it love? She didn't know, but there was no denying that they had a connection, a very strong connection. What if his plan didn't work and she couldn't look at his tattoos? Molly hoped that Jack knew what he was doing.

She heard the bathroom door open and looked toward it. Jack stood watching her. She wondered what he was thinking. Was he thinking the same thing, wondering what would happen if she couldn't look at him?

His hair, still damp from his shower, hung messily, framing his handsome face. The long-sleeved T-shirt he wore stretched across his chest, emphasizing his spectacular pecs. His white boxer briefs left nothing to the imagination, reminding her of what he denied her.

"Why didn't you tattoo your ass? Why did you stop at your waist?"

Jack flicked off the light and made his way to the bed. "That's all the space I needed. I'm not a tattoo junkie, Molly."

She laughed at his sincerity. "You don't think that covering half of your body in tattoos shows signs of addiction?"

"No."

Jack pulled back the covers to find Molly naked under the sheets. He smiled as he climbed into bed. Once settled, he opened his arms, and Molly snuggled into his chest.

"Are you going to elaborate? No isn't an answer."

"How's this for an answer?" Jack asked as he pulled Molly onto his body, covering him from chest to toe. "I didn't cover my body with tattoos because I was saving that honour for you. You are what completes me, Molly Maguire. Having you with me like this, keeping me warm, loving me, is all I need to have on my skin."

"Fuck me."

"No."

"Make love to me then."

Jack chuckled. "No."

She felt his erection press against her belly. Molly desperately wanted to feel him inside her. "How can you say no when I can feel that? I hate you."

"No, you don't."

"How long do I have to wait?"

"It's up to you. It always has been."

She knew he was right. Until she could look at all of him, she wasn't ready to be loved by him. He needed her to see him without seeing his tattoos.

Molly slid off Jack and snuggled into his side with her head resting on his chest. She caressed his torso, feeling the hard outline of every muscle.

"Have you always worked out?" she asked, fighting the need to sleep.

"Yes. Mom made sure we all played at least one sport, and Dad helped us with training. My brother, David, is attending university on a soccer scholarship. Do you play any sports or work out?" Jack asked as his right hand caressed her backside.

"Does my daily walk to the coffee shop count?"

"Definitely."

"Then yes. Will you read me a story?"

"It's time to sleep. Tomorrow we'll read our bedtime story."

"Promise?"

"You know I do."

Jack held Molly and kept the ghosts away. He could listen to her sleep forever, loving the sound of her soft breaths. When he heard her sigh, he hoped it was from dreaming of him. He wondered if Molly knew how much she turned him on. It took every ounce of willpower not to make love to her. Here he was with her sleeping naked beside him, and his erection was still hard. He longed to be inside her, to feel her heat and know that she loved him, but he couldn't. Not until he knew for sure, and she did, too, that she could be with him completely. There would be no more shirts to cover up and no more frosted glass to hide his tattoos from her. When she could see past his ink, then he would show her how much he wanted to love her.

sixteen

Jack awoke to find Molly reading beside him naked. He loved how she was comfortable in her skin, never trying to cover up in his presence.

"Good morning, angel."

"Good morning, dragon slayer. Did you sleep well?"

"Wonderfully well. How about you?"

"No ghosts."

"That's the plan." Jack nodded toward the leather notebook. "You like the stories, don't you?"

"I do. Do you know why?"

"It's the hot sex. Women go for the sex all the time."

"Other than the sex."

"Because you have a crush on my dad, and you can picture him doing everything on every page." Jack put a finger to her temple. "You've got your very own X-rated movie running in your brain when you're reading."

Molly swatted at him. "No. It's because this is our story, too. I get it, Jack. You are my dark knight, and you are rescuing me." She placed the book on her bedside table and then turned her attention back to Jack. "You are right about one thing, though," she said as she scooted down into the bed and faced him. "The stories make me incredibly horny. I want you, now." Her fingers found the waistband of his boxer shorts and tugged at it.

"How much do you want me?" he asked as he pulled her to him, their noses touching.

"Enough that I'll rock your world."

He smiled at her, his blue eyes sparkling with mischief. "I can rock my world, or have you forgotten that I'm a rock star?"

"How about rocking my world then, Mr. Rock Star? Unless you've forgotten how."

"I don't think I'll ever forget how to do that. I learned from the best." He kissed her gently, teasing her mouth with his tongue, and inviting her to open up to him. She returned his kiss, hungry for his taste.

Molly moved closer, grinding her pelvis against his. Her soft moans vibrated in his mouth, encouraging him to take her. There was no ignoring his erection. He was hard and wanted nothing more than to rock her world, but it wasn't in his plans. Not yet. Jack pulled away, groaning as he did so.

"No," Molly pleaded. "Just this once, Jack."

"Can you look at me if I pull this shirt off?"

"I can try."

"Molly. Be honest. Can you look at me, all of me if I take this shirt off?"

"No. Not yet."

"Then we'll wait. Come on. Get up. You owe me breakfast, remember?"

XO XO XO

"What do you love about me?" Molly asked while Jack drove them to Maguire's.

"We've five minutes before we get to your place, so I'll give you the short version."

"Please do."

"I love the way you smile, and that thing you do with your tongue when you lick your bottom lip. It's the sexiest thing going. Give me one of those and I'm yours completely. I love the way your eyes light up when you're talking, especially when you're talking to me, begging me to make love to you. I love the way your ass talks to me—the way you make it move when you know I'm watching you. You know all the right ways to talk to me, angel."

"Not quite. You won't have sex with me even when I beg you."

"Begging is such a turn on."

"You like my ass?"

"I love your ass. That first night when you dropped your raincoat on the floor, and you were naked." Jack sighed with longing. "I could have died then and gone to heaven. Seeing your body with that sweet, rounded ass—"

"You would have died a virgin, Jack."

"Only in body. Every thought about loving you ran through my brain right then. I was happy."

"Why do you call me angel?"

"If you could see how you look when you're asleep in my bed you would know the answer."

XO XO XO

"Are you sure I can't help you?" Jack asked Molly as he leaned against the bar's kitchen counter. He'd never seen anyone create such a mess making breakfast. Even his mother, who wasn't the best cook in the world, didn't come close to the disaster happening in front of him. "Toast is fine, Molly. You must have a toaster somewhere in this kitchen."

Molly blew at the wisps of hair that had fallen in front of her eyes. She wiped her hands on her apron and turned to look at the cause of her cooking fiasco. She could cook. She just couldn't cook while being watched by this hunk of male gorgeousness standing three feet away from her. Especially now when he'd told her how much he loved to watch her ass. "I can cook, you know. I'm fully qualified to be in this kitchen."

"I didn't say you couldn't cook. I only offered to help you."

"That's the problem. You're in here watching me. I need you out of here, Jack. Please wait out in the bar and make yourself useful."

"Useful how?"

"Make coffee. I'm sure you can figure out the coffee machine."

"Are you sure you don't want me here?" he asked her, amused that he was the cause of her mess.

Molly pointed to the door. "Go."

Jack made his way out to the bar and started making coffee. He hadn't told Molly that he had once worked at a bar during his time at university. Another story for her. A lifetime's worth.

Jack pulled out his cell phone and checked his messages. Axl had left a message apologizing once again for coming down with mono. He'd come up with a few songs he wanted Jack to hear, and he hoped they'd see each other soon. Stevie left a message about Mother's Day and told him she'd found the perfect present and that he need not worry about Mom. His dad left several messages, one of them inviting Molly to join them for the big celebration.

Mother's Day was a big Thomas family celebration. His father made sure that his wife was celebrated for giving him the family he adored. Jack smiled when he thought of the lengths his dad went to make the day a special one for his mom. His mother would protest the extravagance lavished on her, although she thoroughly enjoyed the attention. She loved her family and cherished each moment she could spend with them.

Jack glanced toward the kitchen. He would ask Molly if she would come home with him. He realized that she had a mother of her own to celebrate the day with, but maybe he could convince her to change her plans.

Molly backed through the servers' doors carrying two plates full of food. "Breakfast is served," she announced as she placed the steaming plates on the bar counter.

Jack pocketed his cell phone and took a seat at the bar. Molly, noticing that the coffee was ready, poured two cups for them and then joined Jack.

"This looks delicious," Jack said as he cut into the sausage on his plate.

"I thought I'd make you a farmer's breakfast. Hope you like it."

"Mmm," Jack said, nodding his head in approval. "Excellent." He smiled as he thought of Molly in the kitchen. "Do I really make you nervous?"

Molly poured syrup on her pancakes and then shredded them with her knife and fork. She nodded her head yes.

"Are you still nervous?"

"You said you like to watch my ass. How was I supposed to make you breakfast when I knew you were staring at my ass the whole time?"

"I thought you'd like me staring at your ass. You like mine."

"It's not the same."

"How so?"

"It just is."

Jack laughed. "You're right."

Molly smiled appreciatively. "You remembered."

Jack reached for Molly's bar stool and pulled it closer to him. He caged it with his muscular legs and cupped her face with his hands. "I remember everything about you. Never forget that. I know that we haven't been together that long, but I know you."

"And I have so much to learn about you."

"You have a lifetime to get to know me." Jack leaned in and kissed her. It was a soft kiss, warm and tender, filled with promise. "Story time when we've finished eating?"

"Please."

Jack released her, then turned to focus his attention on his breakfast. "We need to do this right," he said before he put a forkful of sausage into his mouth.

"Story time?"

"Yes, but no. We need to get to know each other."

"I thought we were. We've seen each other naked. How much more do we need to know?"

"We need to date. Do what people do to get to know each other."

"So, what are you suggesting?"

"If you can take some time off during the day, we should go out on dates."

"What kind of dates?"

"I don't know. We could go out and catch a movie, go for a walk, grab a cup of coffee—whatever you want."

"I'd like that. When do we start?"

"You're the one working. You let me know."

"I'll talk with Jess. Tomorrow afternoon should work."

"It's a date then."

Molly wouldn't let Jack in the kitchen to help with clean up. She insisted that she could do it much faster without him, and she was right. By the time Jack refilled their coffee cups and settled in her office with his book, she was ready to hear Jack's story.

Jack patted the space beside him on the couch. "Have I told you how much I like this couch? It is so comfy," he said as he stretched out his legs, setting his feet on the coffee table. "It's a great beginning to a wonderful story."

Molly sat beside him and cuddled into his side. "We could try it out again if you'd like."

He accepted the offered cup of coffee and took a sip. "We will, but not right now." Jack reached for his book and read the title aloud. *Jack and Stevie's Bedtime Stories.* Are you ready?"

"Go ahead."

Jack opened the book to its first page. He began to read to Molly, "Once upon a time in a land far away there lived the dark knight and his ladylove."

"Jack, there aren't any words on the page."

"I know. Mom had them made without the words."

"What?"

"Stevie and I knew these stories by heart so much that we changed the characters and the storylines all of the time." Jack fanned the pages of the book for Molly to see. "Only the beginning and the ending stay the same. The story in the middle can be anything we want. Pick any page and you have the next part of your story."

"May I see?" Molly asked, holding her hand out for the book.

Jack gave her the book and watched with keen interest as Molly looked at the pages in wonder.

"This is brilliant, Jack."

"It is, isn't it? Mom's love stories for Dad became his stories for us. Every night he would tell us the adventures of the dark knight and his ladylove. He would change the story, and he would let us make changes, too. The funny part about it was that we would never let Mom tell us the story. It was Dad's story."

"What did she think about that?"

"She said that she found it frustrating, especially when there were times when Dad wasn't around for bedtime, but it made her happy knowing that these stories were our special bond with him. Open the book to any page." Jack smiled when Molly opened to the middle of the book. "Figures. Tell me what you see."

"I see a beautiful castle surrounded by lush gardens and green grass."

"What else do you see?"

"It looks like there's a woman looking out from the tower window. She's waving something."

"What do you think she's doing?"

"I can't see her face. I don't know if she's welcoming someone or trying to get someone's attention to warn them of danger."

"Very good." Jack pointed to the opposite page depicting a knight riding his steed. "What does he tell you?"

"Nothing."

"Nothing? Look again. Tell me what you see."

Molly examined the page. The artwork was captivating. She could see the blue in the knight's eyes and the dimple in his cheeks. His suit of armour was that of a hero—shiny with elaborate detail. His steed was magnificent, shiny black with long hair feathering at his hooves. He gave the impression that he could fly by the way he pranced with knees raised high toward the castle. A dragon's head hung off a strap on the saddle.

"He killed the dragon."

"Go on."

"The woman is welcoming him back. He was triumphant."

"Are you sure about that?"

"Jack, this is what I see. Tell me what you see."

"You are right in that the knight is returning to his castle and his ladylove. She is waving to him, but as a warning that there is danger at the castle. If you look over here," Jack pointed to a window on the far side of the tower, "you'll see flames and at this window there is smoke."

"So, who is in the castle if the black knight has slain the dragon?"

Jack turned the page for her. "The dragon's mate. While the knight went out to kill the dragon, its mate went to kill his."

"That doesn't seem like a very good children's story, Jack. I don't remember this story in my copy of the book."

"I told you this was a special edition. There are only three copies printed."

Molly brought the book to her face for a closer look. "The artwork is incredible. The detail is amazing. Who is the artist?"

"A family friend. Do you like the artwork?"

"Yes, Jack, it's stunning."

"What about this one?" Jack asked as he turned to a full page layout of the dragon.

"Wow. He's beautiful and scary. He's definitely a mean dragon."

"Does he look like Finley?"

"Yes, he does. You have stuffed animals that match your stories?"

"You didn't know?"

"I do now. Will I get the knight? He's pretty hot looking."

"Whatever you want. So, you don't mind how Finley looks?"

"No. He's perfect. Why?" Molly closed the book and let it fall to her lap when she realized the significance of Jack's book. "This is your story, your family pictures. These are your tattoos."

"Yes."

"You said they were a tribute to your family. How can a dragon be a tribute to your family?"

"From the moment my mother conceived Stevie and me, the dragon has always been a part of our lives. No matter what happens to us, we always beat the dragon." Jack shifted and turned so that he could face Molly. "Before I was born, my parents were targets of a very sick man. He tried to kill my father. He tried to kidnap my mother, and when that didn't work, he shot her in the head." Jack took Molly's hands in his. "If you've seen pictures of her, you must have noticed the silver hair at her temple."

Molly nodded. "I thought it was a genetic thing. People get white patches in their hair."

"We call it her dragon's bite. The dragon bit her, and she survived. When Mom was diagnosed with cancer five years ago, I wanted to do something to show I supported her and that she wouldn't be fighting alone. That's when I decided to have her story tattooed on my body."

"Did your mom approve?"

"No, not at first. It's funny. She loves to look at tattoos, and some of her books have heroes with tattoos, but she couldn't stand the thought of any of her children having one."

"I take it your dad doesn't have one."

Jack smiled. "Dad got one about ten years ago. He was in New Zealand filming a war movie and one night he and his cast mates got drunk and decided to get a tribal tattoo. When he returned home, and Mom saw it, she hit the roof. I think it's the only time I have ever seen my mom really mad at my dad."

"Did they fight?"

"Put it this way. Dad had to wear a shirt to bed for months."

"Glad to know I'm not the only one." Molly reached for the book and opened it up. "Jack, your tattoos are a far cry from this picture book. What makes you think that if I like these pictures, I can look at your tattoos? These pictures are storybook pictures for children. Your tattoos are—"

"Identical. There is no difference. Trust me."

"Do you honestly think that it will make a difference? It's not just the tattoos. It's the memory of watching my father being murdered by a man covered in tattoos. It's not a memory that is easy to forget."

"I thought that if you could see mine, then you might forget the ugliness of what you saw when you were eight years old."

"If it were only that easy."

"It could be."

seventeen

It was the lunch hour when Harley entered Maguire's. Harley was a striking woman, drawing the attention of everyone who saw her enter the bar. She was tall and slender with olive skin and thick black hair that fell in cascades to her waist. Her green eyes shone as she looked around the bar. She wore form-fitting black leather pants and a tank top covered by a black leather biker's jacket.

Harley made her way to the bar and sat down on a barstool. She gazed up at the large flat screen television and noticed a Dragon Slayers video playing. She smiled as she watched it. She was in this video. Jack had asked her to play the role of his girlfriend in this one. He said their tattoos would complement each other. The director told them that they had great chemistry in front of the camera, looking like real-life lovers. She wondered what people would say if they knew the truth.

"Hi, may I get you a drink?"

The woman's voice brought Harley out of her reverie. "Oh, hi, I was watching the video. That guy's hot, isn't he?"

Molly looked up at the screen and smiled. "Very." She gazed at Jack before turning her attention back to her customer. "What can I get you?"

"Do you serve burgers?"

"It's one of our specialties. What would you like on it?"

"Lettuce, tomato, mustard and pickle, with a side order of sweet potato fries, if you have them, and I'll have a Coors Lite to go with it. Thanks."

"Coming right up."

Molly placed her order with the kitchen, and then poured Harley her beer. "I haven't seen you in here before. Do you go to the local college?"

Harley smiled. "No. I graduated a few years ago from NYU. I heard about this place, so I thought I'd check it out. I'm on my way to Los Angeles from San Francisco."

"You're taking the scenic route then. This town is out of the way."

"It is," Harley agreed, "but I'm enjoying the sights." She sipped slowly from her glass as she gave Molly the once over. She was pretty. Harley had to give Jack credit for falling for someone with looks. Her skin was perfect. Harley didn't notice a blemish or the mark of a tattoo, although the black T-shirt Molly wore covered up too much skin for Harley's liking. "It's quiet in here. Is it usually like this?"

"It's college exams week. Usually, this place is busy over the lunch hour, but it should be overflowing by this evening. We have a very talented guitarist who is pulling in the crowd."

"Really? Anyone I may have heard of?"

"Jack Thomas of Dragon Slayers."

"I heard the band had to cancel their tour while one of the members recovers from mono. Who gets mono at the age of twenty-five? He must have had his tongue down a lot of throats during the tour. Doesn't surprise me, that band, they're all pigs."

Molly straightened, ready to tackle this woman if she insulted her man. "Jack's not a pig. He's a real sweetheart."

Harley scoffed, "He's the worst of the bunch. Believe me. That man bangs anything on two legs when he's on tour."

"How can you say that?"

"Are you saying he hasn't put the moves on you? You're very pretty, and you're blonde. Jack goes for the delicate looking ones. They don't put up a fight."

"Your burger's probably ready. I'll check for you." Molly didn't wait for an answer as she stormed off to the kitchen. "Where's that burger order?" she yelled. "I want it ready now!"

XO XO XO

Jack noticed the yellow custom Harley Davidson motorcycle parked in front of Maguire's. Only one woman rode a bike with that custom artwork. He entered the bar and noticed her sitting alone on a barstool. There was no mistaking the long black hair or the small leather clad ass perched on the stool. He watched as she stood to unzip her jacket. He knew what Harley wore underneath, and he couldn't let Molly see it. Jack reached her in time. His strong arms enfolded Harley's waist before she took off her jacket.

"What the—" Harley stopped and softened in his arms. "Hey, lover, how are you? I was wondering where you were." Harley turned around and clasped her arms around Jack's neck. She kissed him on the mouth. "Happy to see me?"

Jack smiled at her. "This is a surprise. What brings you out here?"

"I had a job in L.A. and decided to take the bike out for a ride. Stevie said you were hanging out here for awhile, and so I thought it would be nice to drop by and see you. How's Axl? What an idiot."

"He's feeling better. I'll let him know you were asking about him."

"You do that and tell him Stevie is still waiting on that bass line he promised her."

"When did you become Stevie's messenger girl?"

"Since your pal Axl decided not to answer his emails or voice-mails. Sometimes that man can be a real prick."

"I'll talk to him."

Jack looked around and saw Molly watching them from the kitchen door. He released himself from Harley's arms. "Molly, I'd like to introduce you to someone." He could tell that she'd been watching them for some time, and she didn't like what she was seeing.

Molly approached with Harley's lunch order. She set the plate on the bar, all the time staring at Jack. "Do you two know each other?"

"Molly, I'd like you to meet Harley. Harley, this is Molly."

Harley held out her hand. "I knew who you were the moment I saw you. Jack didn't leave out one detail when he described you to me."

Molly took her hand and shook it. "Funny, Jack didn't mention you at all to me."

Jack coughed uneasily. "We haven't talked much about my friends, Molly. We're still getting to know each other."

"You know about Jess."

Harley took her seat at the bar. "You don't mind if I eat my lunch, do you? I'd hate for this to go cold."

"Go ahead," Molly bit out. "Jack's paying for it."

"Jack, are you going to tell Molly about us, or do I have to?" Harley asked before she took a bite of her burger.

"Why don't you tell me, Harley, since Jack seems lost for words."

Harley swallowed before answering, "Jack and I have known each other for about five years. We met through Stevie. You do know who Stevie is, don't you?"

"His twin sister."

"Okay, so he's told you that much. Stevie and Jack studied music, and I studied fine arts at the same university. I was his number one groupie whenever he played on campus, and he attended all of my showings. He even bought a few of my art pieces to keep me in business."

"Get to the point, Harley."

"Yes, get to the point, Harley," Jack said as he made his way round the bar to Molly.

Harley laughed. "You don't think we're lovers, do you?"

"I don't know what to think, to tell you the truth. Watching you kiss him made me wonder."

"Jack is quite the catch, I will admit that, and there were times when I first met him that I thought he might be worth the effort. However—"

"She's Stevie's partner, Molly. Harley is not into men, at least not sexually. She's one of my best friends, and she's my tattoo artist."

"You're the one who marked him?"

"What?"

Jack stared at Molly in disbelief as her words echoed through his head. *She marked you.*

"You put those things on his skin? How could you?"

"Jack?" Harley asked, confused by the accusations.

Jack grabbed Molly's arm as she reached for the baseball bat hanging behind the bar. "Don't even think about it, Molly. Please. Calm down."

"Don't tell me to calm down! I catch you kissing a woman who you want me to believe is your sister's girlfriend. Then I find out she's the one you let use your body as though it were her private colouring book. Don't you think there's something wrong with that story?"

"It's the truth," Jack answered.

"I'm sorry if you think I've done something wrong. Jackie and I have always been affectionate. It's a game we started in university."

"Jackie?"

"Come on, Molly, settle down. The women in my family call me Jackie."

"I don't."

"No, you don't, not yet. Harley's a friend. That's all. There's nothing to be jealous about."

"Do you think I'm jealous?"

"Well, aren't you?"

Molly looked up at Jack with tears in her eyes. "No."

"Then what are you?"

"I'm mad. I'm fucking angry!"

"Over what?"

"Not what. Whom."

Jack reached for Molly.

She stepped back, her eyes opened wide. "Don't touch me."

"Molly, please."

"Another server will look after you. If you'll excuse me, I have work to do."

Jack and Harley watched dumbfounded as Molly walked to her office and closed the door behind her.

"Jack, I'm sorry. I didn't mean to upset her. I wasn't thinking."

"It's my fault. I didn't tell her about you."

Jack poured two shots of Jack Daniels and handed one to Harley. Harley took the offered glass and took a drink.

"I'm a lesbian, is that the problem?"

"No," he shook his head, then took another drink from his glass.

Harley emptied her glass and held it out for a refill. "I have a feeling this is going to be a long story."

"Molly's dad was murdered in this bar by a man covered in tattoos. Molly was eight years old, and she witnessed it."

"Shit."

"She's terrified of tattoos and can't bear to see them on anyone."

"So, what the hell is she doing with you and why is she taking it out on me?"

"We're working on it. That's why I'm here while Axl is out of commission."

"That doesn't explain why she wanted to take a baseball bat to me."

"You're the one who marked me, Harley. She doesn't understand how I could let you do what you did to me, even though it's what I wanted."

"She hates me? Is that it?"

"I think seeing you took her by surprise. She didn't know that you are my friend."

"Not to mention your soon to be sister-in-law."

"What? You and Stevie?" Jack jumped to his feet. "That's fantastic!"

"I haven't asked her yet. I'm waiting for her to finish her tour."

Jack hugged Harley. "She won't say no. She's crazy about you. We're all crazy about you."

"Everyone but your girlfriend."

"I'll talk to her."

"Good luck with that."

Jack released Harley and stepped back from her. "I should check on her."

"And I better get going. I still have a long ride ahead of me." Harley reached into her jacket pocket for her wallet.

"Don't," Jack said as he motioned for her to put it back. "Molly's right. This one's on me."

"Take care," Harley said before she kissed Jack on the cheek. "See you soon."

"Ride carefully."

"Always do."

XO XO XO

Jack knocked on Molly's office door, and when he didn't hear her answer, he entered. He found her lying down on the leather couch clutching the stuffed dragon. Jack closed the door behind him. "Harley's gone."

Jack made his way to Molly. He sat on the coffee table and placed a paper bag on the table beside him. Resting his elbows on his knees, Jack leaned in toward Molly's face and kissed her on her forehead.

"She made fun of you and the band. She called you a pig."

"She was joking. She has a weird sense of humour."

"She's beautiful."

"Yes, she is. She's beautiful on the inside, too. That's why she's a good friend of mine. Stevie is crazy about her. You should see them together. They make the perfect couple."

"I still don't like her. What she did to you was wrong."

"What she did to me was exactly what I wanted her to do to me. You mustn't blame her."

"I can blame her. She should have said no once she looked at your perfect body. She should have known better than to mark you. What kind of person does that?"

Jack straightened, his gaze never leaving her face. "A very skilled and artistic person does that. Harley's the only person I trust to ink me. She cares enough about me and her art to make sure that my tattoos are the best they can be. Did you know that no one else has my tattoos? I own them, and Harley doesn't share the patterns with anyone. There may be knockoffs, but no one knows the technique she used to make them."

"That's supposed to make me like her?"

"Maybe understand her? I wish I could show you her work. You would be amazed."

"Don't push it."

"Would this help?" Jack handed Molly the bag. "I bought this for you this morning."

Molly opened the bag and peered inside. She looked up at Jack, confused.

"Go on, take it out."

"You bought me a doll?"

"Not just any doll, Molly. It's a tattoo doll. You can draw on it." Jack took the bag from Molly and pulled out a package of magic markers. "You draw on it with these."

"What am I supposed to draw?"

"We're going to draw my tattoos on it."

"I don't draw, Jack."

"I'll help you. It doesn't have to be exact. I just want you to get an idea of what this looks like." Jack pointed to his chest. "You've seen the pictures, now let's draw them on this doll."

"You're crazy."

"No. I'm determined and borderline desperate to get you to see what's under this shirt."

"You just want to get laid," she teased.

"Maybe, but you want it more."

Molly opened her mouth to protest, then stopped. "That's not fair."

"But, it's true. I have waited this long for you. I can wait a bit longer. I'm not the one who is begging to get laid."

"I hate you sometimes."

"Maybe, but you love me all of the time."

XO XO XO

"I thought I'd seen everything but seeing you two playing with a doll is a first for me," Jess said from the doorway to Molly's office.

Jack glanced up at her from the leather couch. "Shh, we're at a critical part."

"With a doll?" Jess closed the door behind her and approached the couple. "What are you doing?"

"Molly's drawing my tattoos on the doll."

"Really? I didn't know she could draw."

"I can't," Molly said grimacing as she focused on drawing the scales of the dragon, "but this is good enough."

"May I ask why?"

"Jack had this brilliant idea that if I drew the pictures from this book onto this doll, I would know what his tattoos look like and where they are on his body."

"The idea is that if she knows what she is looking at, then maybe she will be able to look at them on me."

"Did you study psychology, Jack?"

"No."

"I thought so."

"Come on, Jess, have some faith. Jack might be onto something. It's worth trying."

"May I have a look?"

Molly held up the doll for Jess's inspection.

"This is supposed to be Jack?" Jess laughed when she saw the overly large penis drawn on it.

"All Molly's doing," Jack said proudly.

"Right," she said. She noticed Jack had his shirt sleeves rolled up to the elbow. "Living on the edge, Jack?"

"She can cope with this much. We've already established that."

Jess looked back at the doll. Both arms had dark vines running from wrist to shoulder. Shades of black, grey and red formed roses on the vine covering his right arm. On his left arm, there was only one rose, and it was above his wrist.

"Roses?"

"They're Jack's family on his right arm. His left arm is reserved for his future family."

"Your name is on that rose, Molly. That's quite the statement, Jack."

"I think of it as positive thinking," he answered.

Jess knew there was a dragon on Jack's back, and she wondered how Molly managed drawing it. She turned the doll over and nodded her appreciation.

"Nice dragon."

"Just call him Finley. He's not as scary if you call him by his name."

Jack held up his hand when Jess looked up at him. "Her idea, not mine."

"See, Jess, we're working our way through this."

"Well, I hate to break this up, but one of you is expected on stage in ten minutes."

XO XO XO

Jack made his way through the tables to the small stage along the far wall of Maguire's. He liked the positioning of the stage. It gave him the perfect vantage point to watch the blonde bartender. Jack took his seat on the bar stool and accepted the blown kiss she sent his way.

"I want to thank all of you for coming out tonight." Jack waited for the applause and cheers to die down. "I wouldn't be here if it weren't for the very kind invitation of the two lovely ladies tending bar tonight."

There were more cheers for Molly and Jess. Both women waved to the crowd then continued filling bar orders.

Jack strummed a few notes on his acoustic guitar, checking to make sure it was in tune. "As you can see, it's just me playing for you tonight. Axl's on sick leave, Matt's having quality time with his girl-friend, and Ben's working on some new tunes."

Jack played from his heart. He played love songs, all the time gazing toward the bar, making sure Molly knew that he was singing to her. He played acoustic versions of Dragon Slayers hits, giving the songs a softer, more intimate feeling.

"He's killing it tonight," Jess whispered in Molly's ear.

"That he is," Molly agreed.

"Have you noticed his tip jar? It's overflowing."

"Who put that there?" Molly asked. "Do you think he needs the money?"

"It's for the local children's charity. He announced that the first night he played here, and it's on all of his social media accounts."

"He didn't tell me that, but then, we've been busy."

"Colouring." Jess snorted.

"It's working. Tonight, I'm going to ask to see his back."

"Are you sure? Molly, there's no need to rush it."

"I know. Don't worry. I'll be careful."

XO XO XO

Molly watched with interest as Jack spoke with the last of the patrons who had waited for the chance to have a picture taken with him. The woman was beautiful and clearly making a pass at Jack. Molly saw the slip of paper she tucked into his shirt pocket. When the woman turned her back, Molly saw Jack take the slip of paper out of his pocket and let it fall to the floor without looking at it.

She wasn't the jealous type and was proud of it. She never had the time to waste on jealousy. She trusted in a man until he proved himself untrustworthy. If another woman could make him stray, Molly was thankful to let him go. She didn't waste time fighting for a man. She had too much self-respect. She sighed, happy knowing that Jack wanted her. He believed they had a future together.

Molly never had a man try so hard for her before. Men usually assumed they had her love and affection without putting much into the relationship. To be honest, she hadn't put much effort into her relationships either. Until now. Something deep inside her told her that Jack was worth the work. She knew he felt she was worth the effort, too. It didn't escape her either, that Jack understood. The tattoo doll was a brilliant idea. She wasn't jealous of Harley, only mad that Jack had allowed himself to be marked by her. Colouring the doll gave Molly the chance of marking him, too.

"Hey, angel, come back to earth."

"Excuse me?"

"You were off somewhere. What were you thinking?"

"I was thinking of you and me and a doll, and now that you are here, I don't have to think about the doll."

XO XO XO

Jack held Molly's hand as they walked through the hotel lobby toward the elevators. "I'm breaking the rules, you know. Ten demerit points if I'm caught bringing a woman back to my hotel room."

"Band rules?"

"More like a game, but when Axl and Ben brought back more trouble than they could handle, we brought in demerit points."

"What about Matt?"

"His girlfriend would kill him." Jack smiled. "I think they'll be engaged by the time they get home."

"Did you lose points that first time I came to your room?"

"No. I didn't invite you, you weren't a groupie, and you didn't cause trouble."

"I kneed you in the balls." Molly's cheeks reddened from embarrassment at the thought.

"True, but it didn't bother anyone but me, so no loss of points."

"What do you get points for?"

"Nothing embarrassing, if that's what you're asking." Jack pressed the call button for the elevator. "Things like hitting the garbage can with our trash, longest burp, sex with the best-looking groupie—"

"Points for having sex? That's not embarrassing to you?"

"Not to me. I was a virgin. Remember? It's Axl's and Ben's side game."

"Who won?"

"Oh, it's not over. It's a continuous contest."

"Who is in the lead?"

"Probably Axl, although contracting an illness from a groupie cost him 30 points."

The elevator door opened. They entered, and Molly pressed the button for Jack's floor.

"When we were kids, Stevie and I loved elevators. We would ride the hotel elevators and go exploring. We knew our way around every hotel we stayed in."

"You and Stevie went by yourselves? Was that safe?"

"My uncle Jake insisted that one of his security guards go with us. He gave us a long enough leash to explore. We had a lot of fun."

"I can't imagine having security guards."

"They were more like family, Molly. They still are. Sometime, you'll meet them."

Their elevator stopped, and the doors opened. Jack led Molly to his room. Once inside, Jack put his guitar case on the floor and then took Molly in his arms. He pulled her in close and kissed her hard.

"You know what else we liked to do?"

"No," she answered breathless, reeling from his kiss.

"We liked to jump on the beds."

"I'm not jumping on the bed, Jack."

His eyes sparkled at her as he gazed into her eyes. There it was again, that mischievous smile daring her to jump. "I'm not asking you to jump. I want to mess up the bed with you." Jack felt her go limp as her knees weakened beneath her. He held on to her, keeping her upright. "Steady there, love."

"You want to have sex?"

"Desperately, but I promised that I'd wait."

"I didn't make that promise," Molly said. "I want to have sex with you."

"I know, but it's late, and I'm exhausted. I'm suggesting we get in that bed and fool around and fall asleep in each other's arms."

"You call that messing up the bed?"

"Let's give it a try and you can tell me if I'm wrong."

"I had plans for us tonight," Molly said as Jack led her to the bed. "We were going to take a shower together, and I was going to see Finley."

"I know. I couldn't let that happen."

"How did you know?"

"Let's just say a little bird told me and I'm glad she did."

When they reached the bed, Jack pushed Molly gently to make her sit on the edge. He began to undress her, starting at her boots and socks.

"Jess had no right to do that. It's my decision when I can look at you."

"I know, but after the day we've had, I think putting it off is the right choice."

"How can you say that?"

Jack reached for Molly's jeans waistband. He easily popped the button and unzipped her. "I'm not ready for you to look at me."

"Why?" Molly raised her hips to let Jack pull her pants down.

"I have as much to lose as you do, Molly. If you look at my tattoos, and you're not ready, then I run the risk of losing you. I can't take that chance. When the time comes for you to see all of me, we'll both be ready for that day."

He folded her jeans and placed them next to her boots and socks.

"So, until then?"

Jack motioned for her to lift her arms and she obeyed. "We're dating without having sex."

"Your rules, not mine."

"Without the sex," he repeated. Jack pulled her T-shirt over her head, stood back and gazed at her, admiring the matching white lace bra and panties he had uncovered. Jack leaned down and cupped Molly's face in his hands. "There is nothing more important to me than making things right with you. We have a life together waiting for us. We'll get there."

"Why did you undress me?" Molly asked as if suddenly realizing she was almost naked.

"I was speeding along the process of getting you into bed."

"I have to pee and brush my teeth."

"Me, too. Ladies first." Jack stood back and gestured gallantly toward the bathroom.

"Do I get to undress you?"

"Not yet. Hurry up. We have a bed to mess up remember?"

XO XO XO

Molly smiled as she lay beside Jack in his bed. Jack was right. He most certainly knew how to mess up the bed without having sex. Molly may have been the only woman he'd had sex with, but she was damned sure he'd made it to second and third base a few times with someone else. His hands played her. It wasn't touching, more like strumming. Molly closed her eyes, feeling as though she were one of Jack's favourite guitars. His callused fingertips trailed ever so lightly over her abdomen, eliciting the tiniest of shivers from her. His long thumbnail plucked at her nipples. She squirmed in delight. When he kissed her body, he hummed her song to her. The vibrations caused her toes to curl in anticipation.

"You've done this before," she whispered, still breathless from the orgasm his touch had brought.

"Glad to know you think so."

"Don't lie to me, dragon slayer. You've played the bases with some of your groupies."

Jack's chuckle was low and sexy. Molly felt her sex clench in response.

"I don't lie. I can't help it if your body is made for me."

"You said no sex."

"I'm only touching you. Would you like me to stop?"

"No."

"Is there something you'd like me to do that I may have overlooked?"

"Yes. Fuck me."

There it was again. That low sexy chuckle that promised every divine sin she could imagine. "No."

"I hate you."

"Yes, you've told me before. Lucky for you I know you're lying." Jack kissed her. His kiss was hot, tasting of his cinnamon-flavoured toothpaste. She loved the taste of cinnamon. His tongue traced the outline of her top lip and then her bottom lip. He nipped it and then licked it again. "You taste so sweet, love."

"You haven't tasted everything."

"I know." Jack pulled Molly onto him. He cupped the cheeks of her ass and massaged them.

"Don't you want to taste all of me, dragon slayer?"

"You know I do. Another time."

"May I taste you?" She moved against him, enjoying the feeling of his erection pressing against her.

"Another time. We need to sleep."

"I hate you."

"Sweet dreams, angel."

eighteen

She came to him in his dreams. He hadn't dreamed of his mother
in quite some time. Jack remembered this dream. He had dreamed it
many times before. His mother had taken him and Stevie to the park
to play. David, still a baby, was in his mother's arms. They played to
their hearts' content. They swung on the swings, played tag on the
climbers, and tried the seesaws. When it was time to leave, his mother
bought them popsicles and then they went home.

This dream was different. When it was time to go home, the sky
darkened as though a storm had appeared unexpectedly. Jack could
feel the wind against his face. It was hot and reeked of bitter smoke.
Jack looked for signs of fire, but there was only smoke around him, no
flames. His eyes stung from the smoke, and he cried out. He grabbed
Stevie's hand, and they searched for their mother. Then suddenly the
air cleared around them, and the dragon swooped down and took
hold of his mother with its massive talons. His mother's legs dangled
in front of Jack. He grabbed her feet and hung on for his life. She
yelled at him to let go before the dragon carried both of them away.
Jack let go, falling to the ground.

He awoke in a sweat. His heart pounded against his chest, and he
felt a weight pressing him into the mattress. It took him a moment to
realize that it was Molly. Her head nestled against his chest, with her

left arm and leg draped over his body. Jack wrapped his arm around her and held her close for the longest time. Her quiet breaths and the touch of her soft skin calmed him. Jack looked at his watch. He could call home. His Mom was always up at this time.

Jack moved Molly to his side, taking care not to disturb her. He slipped out of bed, taking his cell phone with him into the bathroom, then shut the door before he turned on the light.

"Jack."

"Dad?" Instantly, Jack knew that something was wrong. "I dreamed about Mom. It scared the hell out of me. Is she okay?"

"Jack, she's had an accident. You'd better come home."

Still reeling from the news about his mother, Jack went into auto-pilot. He gathered his toiletry bag from the bathroom and dropped it into his full suitcase. One rule of the tour was never to unpack. The clothes he wore earlier lay on the top of the bag. Jack dressed then gathered up his car keys and cell phone. He'd almost forgotten Molly was sleeping soundly in his bed. He didn't dare wake his sleeping angel. He was too upset to speak.

Jack wrote a note instead, *Molly—I'm sorry. I have to go. Jack.* He left the note on her pillow. He gathered up his suitcase and guitar, took one last look at Molly and left.

The next few hours were a blur to him. Jack made his way back to L.A. and made arrangements for Ben to meet him at the airport to take his car. Harley called him to confirm that she had booked tickets for both of them to fly to Toronto and that she would be waiting for him at the airport.

Harley and Ben met Jack when he pulled up to the departure area. Ben hugged him and uttered words of support. Jack didn't register them. He grabbed his suitcase and let Harley lead him through the airport. He was thankful that he had her with him.

"Jack?" Harley asked him once they settled into their seats on the airplane.

"Huh?"

"She'll be okay. Your mom's a fighter."

"I know."

"Does Molly know?"

"I think so."

"What do you mean?"

"I left her a note on her pillow. I think I explained everything to her. She looks like an angel when she's sleeping. I didn't have the heart to wake her."

"You have time. Give her a call."

Jack reached into his jacket pocket and then his pants pocket. "Damn it. I must have left my phone in my car."

Harley handed Jack her cell phone. "Use mine."

"I don't know her number. Do you have Ben's number on yours?"

"Yes."

Jack found Ben's number and pressed dial. The call went directly to his voicemail.

"Ben, it's Jack. I left my cell phone in my car. Will you please courier it to my parents' address in Canada? If you need to contact me, call Harley. Thanks." Jack ended the call.

"You don't know her number?" Harley asked.

"Soon to be rectified."

"Why don't you have Ben call Molly? It could take a while before you get your phone."

"What would I do without you?" Jack called Ben again. "Ben, do me a favour and call Molly. Tell her I've had to go home for a family emergency, and I'll call her when I can. Thanks." Jack ended the call and handed the cell phone to Harley.

"That was better, but you should have woken her up."

XO XO XO

Molly stretched, more asleep than awake. She had a wonderful dream about Jack. He made love to her. Finally. Molly smiled, remembering how shocked she was in her dream that he finally agreed to it. Her hand went to her mouth and touched her lips. She could still feel his mouth against hers, kissing her and coaxing her to give more. Molly sighed. She felt the ache between her legs. She touched herself, hoping to find something to let her know he had been with her. Nothing.

She rolled over to her side and reached out. Jack's space was empty and cold. Molly opened one eye and then the next as she realized that she was alone.

"Jack?"

The silence and the darkness of the room caused a shiver to run up her spine.

"Jack, are you here?"

Molly scrambled out of bed and opened the bathroom door. He wasn't there, and neither was his toiletry bag. She went back into the room and turned on the lights. Jack's departure became painfully clear. Molly rubbed at the ache in her chest. How could he leave her? She saw the note on her pillow. Molly raced to the bed and grabbed it.

Molly read the note aloud, "Molly—I'm sorry. I have to go. Jack." Molly crumpled the note and cried.

XO XO XO

It was a relief to Jack to see his Uncle Jake waiting for them at the airport. Jake was as big as a bear and could be just as fierce when pushed, but he was always playful and kind with Jack and his siblings. Jake was his father's best friend and owned the security company that had always been in charge of protecting the Thomas family.

"Jack. Harley. I wish it were happier reasons bringing you here."

Jake hugged Jack and then Harley. He escorted them out of the airport to their waiting limo. Jake put their luggage into the trunk and then joined Jack and Harley in the back of the limo.

"How is she?"

"I think she should be released, and your dad should be the one in the hospital. He's taking her accident harder than she is."

"That's Mom."

"She broke both her right leg and wrist. She's got lots of bruises and a mild concussion. She's lucky she didn't break her neck."

"Is it true she fell down the stairs?" Harley asked.

"She tripped over the cat."

Jack shook his head. "That damned cat. Mom always said if we found her dead at the bottom of the stairs that it would be the cat's fault. How's the cat?"

"I think she's in hiding. Quinn would have killed her if he had the chance. Davi threatened to leave him if he did."

"She does love her pets," Jack admitted. "Has anyone else made it home?"

"It looks like we'll be running a shuttle service today. Stevie's flight is on schedule. She'll arrive later tonight."

"Will you take us directly to the hospital?"

"That's the plan."

XO XO XO

Her calls went straight to his voicemail. Texts went unanswered. Molly didn't have Jack's email address. She paced in her office, thinking the worst and hoping that Jack would walk through her door at any moment. Other than that damned note, there had been no word from him. When Molly checked with the hotel clerk, Jack had paid the bill and left nothing else for her.

Jess walked in and headed to Molly's desk. "You'll want to see this," she said as she clicked on the laptop's browser and opened a popular celebrity news website. "Jack got on a plane."

"What?" Molly asked as she made her way to look at the screen.

She watched with horror as the video clip from an online celebrity gossip site showed Jack making his way through the airport with a woman on his arm. Harley. They weren't smiling, but they didn't look unhappy either. Jack was his usual gorgeous self, wearing jeans, white shirt and leather jacket. His hair was fashionably messy. Harley looked as though she had just stepped out of a fashion magazine dressed all in black—leather moto jacket, cropped shirt, and pencil skirt, with killer heels. And her hair—long straight black hair that fell to her waist. The hairs on Molly's neck stood on end. Jack and Harley were a couple.

"That lying son of a bitch!"

"Molly, you don't know that. You don't know what they're doing at the airport or where they are going."

"His note didn't say he'd be coming back, Jess. It didn't say that he loved me. He only said he was sorry. He's left me for her. Maybe he was always with her. When she dropped by the bar, she was checking me out. Probably having a laugh about how gullible I was to think I had a chance with Jack."

"He's crazy about you. If he weren't, he wouldn't have come back here."

"Maybe being crazy about me wasn't enough. All it took was that woman showing up here and reminding him of what he was missing for him to leave me. I guess I was too much work. I was taking too long to get over his tattoos. Look at them," she said pointing to the screen, "They're the perfect couple. They belong together."

Jess shook her head. "I don't believe it. You're jealous."

"I don't do jealous. I dump men before I have to go through that."

"You don't do jealous because you don't want to invest yourself in a relationship."

"I don't know what you're talking about." Molly turned away and walked to the leather couch. She sat down and picked up the stuffed dragon, pretending to examine every detail of its plush body.

"All of the guys you've dated weren't half the guy Jack is. It was easy to let them go because you knew they weren't worth the effort. I understand that. Jack's different. I'll admit that I thought it was a dumb-assed idea for you to try to have a relationship with him, but he's a keeper. Molly, if you let him go, the blame will be on you, not him."

"That's not true. He left me."

"He left, but you don't know if he left you. Give him the benefit of the doubt. At least try. You know I'm right. I've known you for what feels like forever. You want the happily ever after. You want the husband, the house with four kids and the picket fence. But when it's time to put in the extra effort with a guy, you find an excuse to dump him, and you bail."

"I do not."

"You do. You thought Curtis was cheating. You thought Pat should get a better job, and you thought John was dating you to get free drinks at the bar."

"He was dating me for the free drinks. All of our dates ended up here and then he left at last call."

"Jack's not cheating on you, and he's not with you for the free drinks. He's trying his damnedest to help you with your fear of tattoos. Would a guy who didn't care about you put in all of the time and effort to help you? Do you honestly think he's the type of guy to walk away?" Jess got to her feet and headed toward the door. "On second thought, you might be right. It takes one to know one, and you sure as hell know how to walk away."

Molly threw the dragon at Jess. "Why are you such a bitch to me? You're supposed to be on my side."

Jess caught the dragon. "I am on your side. That's why I'm trying to get you to face the facts."

"What facts?"

"You are a terrible girlfriend. You're stubborn, you're quick to judge, and you think you're always right. No more excuses, Molly. You have the chance to be a great girlfriend for Jack. It's up to you if he stays or leaves. No one else."

Jess threw the dragon back at Molly before opening the door and leaving Molly alone.

"He's the one who left!" Molly shouted. "And I am always right. You just don't know it yet!"

nineteen

Jack sat by his mother's bedside. He held her hand while singing Molly's song to her, trying unsuccessfully to block out the ticking and beeping sounds of the hospital monitors attached to her.

"Jack's written a beautiful song for his girlfriend, hasn't he, love?" Jack's father asked his wife.

"It's lovely, Jackie."

"Jack, tell us more about Molly. We were talking about you and Molly when she—" Quinn took a deep breath to steady his nerves. "When she tripped over that damned cat. Now she has you here to give her all of the details."

Jack knew his father was a great actor. However, he could never wear his Hollywood face when it came to his wife. The strain and fatigue from worry were visible for everyone to see. He hadn't left his wife's side since her admittance to the hospital. Only Quinn's blue eyes had the same sparkle he reserved for the love of his life. They were a constant in the love story they shared with their family.

"She's beautiful, Mom. I call her my angel. She has blonde hair and blue-grey eyes that pull me in and keep me riveted."

"It's always the eyes, isn't it?"

Jack saw how his mother gazed at his father and smiled.

"She's stubborn, and she told me that she will always be right no matter what."

"Women are always right, Jack," his father agreed. "You'd better get used to it now. Your life will be a lot easier once you do."

"We're always right because we are right," Davina said. "How is she with your tattoos? Did you tell her your story?"

"I did. We were making progress, Mom. I bought her a tattoo doll."

"A tattoo doll?"

"Yes. It's a cloth doll that you can draw on to get an idea of what your ink will look like on your body. You can figure out the placement and the colouring."

"You did what with it exactly?"

"I showed her my storybook and told her my tattoos matched the drawings, and then I marked where they were on my body. Molly drew them on the doll and coloured them in. I thought that if she did the work, she'd get used to them and maybe accept them when she saw them on me."

"Has she seen any of them?" his father asked.

"She's seen my arms. I got this one for her." Jack rolled up his sleeve on his left arm and showed his parents.

"That's commitment," his mother remarked.

"Foolish, too. What if it doesn't work out with her, son? You've got that woman's name on your arm forever."

"It will work out with her, Dad. I know it will. When I left her, we were in a good place. She was close to seeing me. She wanted to. Molly's very impatient. It's very hard saying no to her."

"It always is."

"When have you ever had to say no?" Davina asked her husband.

"I can't remember."

"You can't remember because it has never happened. Jack, don't listen to your father. He's not the world's expert on women."

"I don't have to be an expert on all women, Davina Stuart Thomas. I only have to be an expert where you are concerned. I think my twenty-five years with you have proven me right."

"I think you need a few more years to be sure."

"I'll take as many years as I can get." Quinn rose from his chair and leaned over to kiss his wife. "I love you so damned much."

"I know. I love you, too."

Jack smiled. He loved being with his parents and witnessing their loving banter. "And on that note, I think I'll head home and get a shower. You two look like you need some alone time." Jack got to his feet, leaned over his mother and kissed her on the forehead.

"Jackie?"

"Yes, Mom?"

"I dreamed about you. Were you dreaming about me?"

"What did you see, Mom?"

"You were keeping me here on this earth. The dragon had me and you grabbed me by the feet and pulled me free. Is that what you dreamed?"

"I let go, Mom. I couldn't hold on."

"You let go once I was safe, Jack. You held on long enough."

"I love you, Mom."

"Always and forever, Jackie."

XO XO XO

Jack wasn't one for making use of limousines, but in this instance, he was thankful that his Uncle Jake had made one available for shuttling the family from the farm to the hospital. His mind was too much on his mother to allow him to drive home safely. He closed his eyes and dozed.

It bothered him that he dreamed that he let go of his mother, and yet in her dream he saved her. The realness of his dream was still with him, and he felt a cold sweat start under his shirt. *I let her go.* Jack had dreams of his parents before, however, nothing quite like this one. As a child, he would wake up in his bed and find his mother sitting next to him, watching over him. Somehow, she always knew when he was dreaming about her. She would comfort him by saying, *I know Jack. It's okay. I know.*

When Jack was eleven or twelve, his Aunt Maggie visited him. It wasn't unusual for her to drop by with freshly baked muffins or cookies. This time, she brought Jack's favourite, chocolate chip cookies. Maggie made tea for them, putting milk and sugar in Jack's since he hadn't quite acquired a taste for the brew. They sat at the kitchen table and talked about everything and anything. Maggie always had the gift of gab.

Then she asked him, "Will you tell me about your dreams?"

At first, Jack denied having dreams that were worth telling. He said they were about being a rock star or doing something crazy with one of his siblings. He even made up dreams so that he wouldn't have to face the truth. His dreams scared the hell out of him.

"Let me tell you something, young man. You have dreams that are very special. Did you know that your mother has the same dreams? Don't you think it a coincidence that you wake up and find her sitting at your bedside?"

"I thought she could hear me having a nightmare."

"No, Jack, that's not why. Since you were a baby growing in your mother's womb, you have come to her in her dreams. You have told her things that proved to be true."

"No, I haven't."

"When Davina was in her coma, you came to her and told her that she was going to have you and Stevie. You even named Stevie in the dream."

"Mom, told me that, but I thought it was just a story."

"It's true. Before David came to live with you, you had dreams about him. You told your mother that a baby was coming. That you were getting a baby brother."

"I don't remember that."

"I know. You were only four at the time. You knew about your mother's cancer scares and told her she would be fine. You are a comfort to your mother, Jack, and you always will be."

"I thought it was our stories. I always saw a dragon in those dreams, and I explained them as being my crazy imagination."

Jack's Aunt Maggie had psychic abilities. Before Jack and Stevie were born, she could foretell Davina's future. Once the twins were born, her abilities focused on them, and Jack's dreams were her only signs of the future. Maggie had no explanation for Jack's dreams, only that they were a gift that should be accepted and used wisely.

Jack felt the motion of the limousine stop. He opened his eyes and saw the familiar sights of home. They were at the security gate that led up a tree-lined laneway to the farmhouse. He remembered when he and Stevie would race each other to the gate to catch the school bus. They always tied. His mother's gardens bloomed with colourful spring flowers. He knew his mother planted every bulb. She loved her gardens.

Once at the farmhouse, Jack let himself out of the limo. He didn't expect service. He could look after himself. "Are you coming in?" he asked the driver, not knowing what the plan was.

"No, thank you. I'm off to the airport. Your sister's flight is due to arrive soon."

"Okay. Thanks for the ride."

As soon as he stepped inside the farmhouse kitchen, Jack felt comfort in the smells of home. There was the aroma of freshly brewed coffee and a plate of chocolate chip cookies placed on the kitchen table. A note lay on the table beside it. Jack picked it up and read it. *I'll check in with you tomorrow, love Maggie.* He smiled and helped himself to a cookie.

Jack noticed his suitcase and guitar case by the kitchen door, dropped off when Harley came back to the house earlier. He took two more cookies from the plate then walked to his mother's office. He opened the door, flipped the light switch and stood in the doorway, looking at her desk, imagining her sitting there working at her computer. She would always smile at him and invite him to sit in his father's chair directly across from her desk. Jack would take his seat and then they would talk. They talked about anything and everything. His mom made sure she kept current with the music scene, and Jack always had a bad joke he'd heard or read on the internet. They talked about life, family and love.

He entered her office. He noticed the notes she had on her desk. A quick glance told him she was writing another book about the farm. She loved to write about the farm and her cows that she lovingly called the Ladies. Jack made his way to Davina's photo wall. Sometimes he would find her in her desk chair staring at the family pictures and smiling.

"It's almost complete," she would tell him. "Everyone has a partner and a family. It's just my little ones who need to finish it."

She called Jack, Stevie, and David her little ones. It made sense since her children from her first marriage were close to his father in age. Her first marriage produced three children: Cat, Rich and Tigger. It lasted twenty-five years until her husband died in his sleep.

Two years later, a new family began, a result of a chance meeting on an airplane and love at first sight. The two sets of offspring were the perfect blend. The eldest spoiled the youngest, and the youngest thought their older siblings were the best brother and sisters a kid could want.

Stevie and Harley had been a couple for five years. Jack was sure Stevie would say yes once Harley popped the question. He and Molly would one day be on the wall. He knew it in his heart. And David? He was too young to settle down, and as far as Jack knew, his little brother was still enjoying the college dating scene.

Jack's body ached, and all he could think of was a hot shower and bed. He would call Molly tomorrow and tell her everything.

XO XO XO

He felt the soft tickle on his ear and hot breath against the back of his neck. "Jackie, wake up. Come on, big brother, wake up." Even though he was only two minutes older than her, Stevie always thought of him as her big brother.

"What time is it?" Jack asked, more asleep than awake.

"It doesn't matter. Wake up and talk to me."

"Stevie," Jack groaned as he turned onto his back. "Shouldn't you be in bed with Harley having hot sex or something like that?"

She poked him in the shoulder. "Shut up. We have to talk first."

Jack rubbed his hands over his face. "Okay, I'm listening."

"Did you see it happening?"

He knew what she meant without asking. "Yes."

"Why didn't you warn her? Mom could have died for fuck's sake."

"I don't have any control over it. I see things when I'm meant to see them. I'm not a fortune teller."

"So, you knew Mom hurt herself."

"I thought she died."

"You saw her die?"

"No. I saw the dragon take her away, and when I tried to pull Mom away from him, I let go. I thought she died."

"Oh, Jackie."

"It scared the hell out of me. I've never been as scared as I was when I woke up from that dream. If it hadn't been for Molly sleeping with me, I don't know how I would have calmed down."

"Molly? Your girlfriend?"

"Yes."

"She hates my girlfriend. Not cool, Jackie."

"She doesn't hate Harley. She doesn't like it that Harley's the one who inked me."

"Jealous?"

"No. She hates that someone would do that to me. She hates my tattoos, Stevie."

"Then why are you with her? Find someone who appreciates that manly body of yours. I know you've got a lineup of admirers around the world. They're crazy about you in Budapest."

"She's the one for me, little sister. I can't let her go."

Stevie wished that she could see her brother's eyes in the darkness. His eyes always mirrored his feelings.

"You had sex with her, didn't you?"

"Yes."

"She popped your cherry, and now you're in love with her? Big brother, it doesn't have to be that way."

"I fell for her first, and then I let her pop my cherry. And by the way, she thought I lied to her about that. It seems that I know what I'm doing when it comes to sex."

"You told her? Why?"

"It just came out."

"I'm sure it did."

"Don't you have a girlfriend waiting for you?"

"Okay, I'm going. To be continued, Jackie."

"Fine. Just let me get some sleep."

"Mom's going to be okay, isn't she?"

"Yes. Now leave me alone. We'll talk in the morning."

twenty

Jack found the telephone number for Maguire's on Google. He called the bar and was disappointed to get its voicemail. Not knowing who would hear the message, he kept it brief, "Hi, it's Jack. I don't have my cell phone, and I'll be hard to reach. Please tell Molly I'll call her when I can."

"That was romantic," Harley teased from the office doorway. "Couldn't you at least borrow a line from one of your dad's movies, your mom's books, or one of your songs?"

"It's the bar's voicemail. I don't know who will be listening to it."

"Men."

"What about men?" Stevie asked as she peered over Harley's shoulder.

"Everything," Harley said. "Who's making breakfast?"

"Pancakes?" Jack asked.

"You read my mind, Jackie."

"Tell us about your crazy girlfriend," Stevie said while she made the coffee.

"She's not crazy," he answered as he stood watching over the pancakes on the griddle.

"She threatened my girlfriend with a baseball bat. You don't think that's crazy?"

"Stevie. Nothing happened. Give it a rest," Harley pleaded.

"No. Jackie's involved with a wacko who has a pretty short temper. I would say that's something to be concerned about."

"She apologized for how she behaved. I'm sure she'll apologize to Harley if given the chance."

"Not good enough, big brother," Stevie said as she shoved a plate at him.

Jack filled the plate with the cooked pancakes and then added more batter to the griddle.

"If you can sing while you play the guitar, you can talk while you cook, Jack. It's not that hard."

Jack laughed. He loved his sister's smart mouth. Everyone who loved her knew that her bark was worse than her bite.

"Meeting Harley was a shock to Molly. Molly has a hard time dealing with the idea that I would allow someone to tattoo me."

"I told you she was crazy!"

Jack added the rest of the cooked pancakes onto the plate and then nodded toward the kitchen table.

"Let's eat. You can't talk as much with your mouth full."

They joined Harley at the table. Jack knew that Stevie wouldn't drop the subject of Molly. Stevie was like a dog with a bone. She never let go. Once she had covered her pancakes in butter and maple syrup, she'd be on his back again.

It was Harley who broke the silence. "I've been thinking about what you told me about Molly, Jack. I understand where her head is at."

"You aren't serious," Stevie argued.

"Let me speak, please."

Harley and Stevie gazed into each other's eyes. Jack watched as Stevie's facial expression softened from anger into love. Jack smiled.

"I'm sorry. Continue."

"Molly sees your tattoos as marks or scars, correct?"

"Yes. She's trying to understand why I've done this to myself, and it's even harder for her to understand why I would let anyone do this to me."

"Your tattoos are beautiful, Jackie. Don't let her make you think they aren't."

"I don't and I never will."

"So, Molly's reasoning for wanting to hit me was avenging what I did to you."

"That's stupid," Stevie muttered under her breath.

Harley held up her finger to signal she had more to say, "What if she went after me because she's jealous?"

"She knows you and Stevie are a couple."

"I know. It's not that kind of jealousy. You and I have a special relationship that only we can share, one based on trust, and it has an intimacy no one else can have. She said I marked you, correct?"

"Yes."

"When I mark you, you trust me to do the best that I can do. You have complete faith in me to know what I'm doing."

"You're the best," Stevie beamed.

Harley smiled her thanks. "It's the intimacy that we share that she can't have with you. You let me touch you, Jack, in a way that no one else is allowed." She held out her hands to him. "These hands touched you and left their mark on you for everyone to see. There's no hiding that."

"I didn't see it like that."

"You're not a woman, big brother."

Jack got up from the table to get the coffee pot. As he refilled everyone's cup, he thought about Molly's name on his wrist. He put the coffee pot down on the table and exposed his left arm to Stevie and Harley.

"What about this? She loves that I have her name on my wrist."

"I told you. She's crazy."

"Stevie, be serious." Harley continued, "You've shown her your commitment to her. That's damned romantic if you ask me."

"And beautiful," Stevie chimed in.

"Molly wants to get over her fear of tattoos. She wants to be able to see all of me. We were making progress."

"How were you making progress? What's your method, big brother?"

"We read *Jack and Stevie's Bedtime Stories*."

Jack didn't have to say anything else. Stevie knew the stories and the book as well as her brother did. She knew every picture and story they imagined. She had the same mischievous smile as her brother, and it appeared instantly on her face when she heard his answer.

"Brilliant. Give her the stuffed dragon. Girls love the dragon."

"Is it the same one you won't travel without?" Harley teased.

"She's got the dragon, and she's named him Finley."

"Cool," Stevie said. "Maybe she's not as crazy as I thought."

XO XO XO

Molly listened to the voicemail three times. Jack left no explanation for his absence, no number where she could reach him, and no I love you when he said goodbye.

"It's over," she said to Jess. "He would have said something to let me know why he left."

"It's the bar's voicemail. Maybe he didn't want to leave anything personal or embarrassing that the staff would hear."

"You and I are the only ones who check the messages. Don't give me that for an excuse."

Jess walked over to the couch and picked up the stuffed dragon. She rubbed its ears and made funny faces at it.

"He wouldn't give you Finley and just walk away."

"He would if he had someone like Harley waiting for him."

"She's a lesbian, Molly."

"She didn't look like one to me."

"Oh, I forgot. You have the best gaydar in the world."

Molly stuck out her tongue at Jess. She hated it when Jess argued with her. It usually meant Jess was right.

"I'd leave me if I were him."

"Not this again. I'm sorry for what I said."

"You were right. I haven't made anything easy for Jack. I'm too hot-headed. Threatening to hit Harley with the baseball bat could have been what sent Jack running."

"You did what?"

"When I found out she was responsible for his tattoos, I lost it and went for the bat. Jack stopped me. I wouldn't have hit her. I know I wouldn't. It just pissed me off knowing that she was the one who did it."

"Oh, honey. That was crazy."

"Tell me about it."

Molly snatched the dragon from Jess and hugged it tight. She missed Jack. She hated not knowing where he was or why he had to leave her suddenly. She hated how his absence was affecting her; the constant ache in her heart and nausea that lasted most of the day.

XO XO XO

Stevie hooked her arm through Jack's as they made their way to their mother's hospital room and whispered in his ear, "She'll be ready to kill Dad. He hasn't left her side."

"She'll be fine. Trust me. I saw how they were looking at each other. Dad's here until she gets released."

"You're always on Mom's side."

"It's not a matter of picking sides. You don't watch them. You don't see how they are with each other. He's not leaving her."

They stopped outside of her room. Jack knocked on the door.

"Come in."

Stevie pushed past her brother and headed for her mother. "Mom!" she cried out when she saw the casts on her leg and arm.

"I'm fine," Davina said, her face reddening from embarrassment. "Did you see Kitty? Is she okay?"

"She's fine. I found her under my bed. She had her toys with her," Stevie said as she bent over to hug her mother.

"Make sure she's eating, okay?"

"I won't mind if she starves," Quinn grumbled as he stood to greet his family.

"Daddy, be nice. You know you love that cat just as much as Mom does."

She made her way over to her father and hugged him. "How are you? Are you ready to come home?" Stevie scrunched her nose. "You need to have a shower and get some sleep, Daddy. You're starting to smell. I'm sure Mom's ready to kick you out."

"I'm good."

"No, Daddy, you're not. You need the break and Mom does, too. I'm right, am I not, Jack?"

Jack kissed his mom and winked at her. He could see the sparkle in her eyes. Davina was enjoying the concern her daughter was showing. "How are you, Mom? How's your pain? Are you getting enough meds?"

"I'm fine. My doctor was just here. I'm going home today."

"Are you sure you should come home, Mom? You should get your rest."

"Your mother is fine, Stevie. Her bed is waiting for her, and I will be tending to her every need. We've got this."

"When do you think you'll be released?"

"Sometime around lunch. Go home," Davina said to them. "We can visit then."

"We'll have lunch ready for you," Jack offered.

"Have you spoken to Molly since you've been home? How is she?"

"I haven't been able to reach her."

"Make sure you talk to her, Jack. Let her know that you are thinking of her."

twenty-one

Jack's cell phone arrived by courier five days after he had asked Bob to send it to him. While he charged the battery, he checked his phone for voicemail and texts. He was surprised and disappointed to find that Molly had called several times but had not left one message. Her texts were only two words, "Call me."

He pressed speed dial for her number and then waited for her to pick up. Her phone went to voicemail. Jack killed the call. He texted, "Please call me. I have my phone. We need to talk." He called Maguire's. His call went to voicemail.

"No luck?" Stevie asked him when she saw the disappointment on his face.

"She's not taking my calls."

"Maybe she's had time to think about you and realized she doesn't want you. Women do that. Trust me."

Jack shook his head. "We were working on trust. I thought we almost had it."

"Trust for what?"

"She is supposed to trust that I'm telling her the truth, and I'm trusting in her to learn to like my tattoos."

"Why would she think you would lie to her? You couldn't tell a lie to save your life."

"You know that, but she doesn't. She's been lied to by her exes. And—"

"And what?"

"And she found it hard to believe that I wasn't living the life of a rock star."

"Ha!" Stevie leaned back in her chair. "She thought you should be screwing everything on two legs? Is she disappointed that you don't do drugs? Give me a break."

"You're not very sympathetic."

"You're right. I'm not. If Molly can't accept you for the man that you are, then it's her loss, not yours. I know I haven't met her, but Harley has. First impressions mean a lot, Jack, and I'm not impressed by what I've heard about her."

"You just have to get to know her. She doesn't like surprises and she doesn't like —"

"Men with tattoos and she doesn't like tattoo artists. Yada yada."

"When did you become so cynical?"

"I'm not cynical. I'm protective. I don't like it when someone doesn't like my brother, and I don't like it when someone doesn't like your tattoos, especially since they are a work of art."

"By a certain someone."

"Especially since they were done by a certain someone. And I don't like it when someone gives my brother the brush off. You can do better, Jack. Walk away while you still can."

Jack's cell phone rang. He answered it on the first ring. "Hello?"

"Jack, it's Axl. You have to save me. I'm going crazy doing nothing. To hell with doctor's orders, we're going back on tour."

"Axl—"

"I've got it all worked out. I called the guys; management is on board. I signed a waiver releasing the band from all responsibility. It's a go, Jack. Pack your bags. We play tomorrow."

XO XO XO

"Go," his mother told him. "I'm fine, and I have your father to look after me. Stevie and Harley are here for a few more days, and everyone else is scheduling their visits. It will be the longest Mother's Day celebration I've ever had."

"I forgot about Mother's Day."

"We had our visit, Jackie. I couldn't ask for more. You have the chance to do what you love to do. Don't let it pass you by."

"Are you sure?"

"Yes."

"I love you, Mom."

"I know, and you know that I love you, too. I wouldn't tell you to go if I thought you should be here. The band needs you right now, and that's where you should be."

XO XO XO

"Molly?" Jess asked from behind the closed bathroom door. "Are you alright? You've been in there a long time."

"Go away," Molly called out. "Leave me alone."

"Not when you sound like that. Tell me what's wrong." She knocked on the door. "Tell me what's going on, or I swear I will kick this door down."

Jess heard grumbling and then unlatching of the lock. "Finally! Molly, what's—"

"It's positive," Molly said as she held out the pregnancy test stick to Jess. "I'm pregnant."

Molly leaned against the wall and slid down to sit on the floor.

Jess joined her. She looked at the indicator, then at Molly. "You can take another test."

"This is the second one. They both came out positive."

"I thought you were on the pill."

"I am. I didn't miss a day. I swear it. I didn't miss one pill." Molly held her head in her hands and sighed. "We only had sex twice, Jess."

"I don't think the number of times matters, honey."

"He was a virgin!"

"That doesn't matter either. Even if you were a virgin, you could still get pregnant."

"What am I going to do?"

"What do you want to do?"

"Make a doctor's appointment."

XO XO XO

She was six weeks pregnant. Molly rubbed at the ache in her heart. It hadn't left her since Jack left her weeks ago. It pained her every time she read a text from him or saw his number on her call display. She changed her phone number and told Jess not to take his calls. Soon he stopped calling Maguire's.

"What are you going to do?" Jess asked her.

"Nothing. I need time to think. Mind looking after this place while I take some personal time and visit my mom?"

"Sure. Take all the time you need. What about Jack?"

"I think he's out of the picture, wouldn't you agree?"

"He has a right to know, Molly."

XO XO XO

"You're an idiot!"

Jack looked up from his laptop to see Axl staring down at him.

"There is a parking lot out there filled with gorgeous babes waiting to service you and you're in here hiding?"

"I'm not hiding. I'm just not interested in meeting anyone at the moment."

"Who said anything about meeting them? Go out there, look at them, and then put your arm around the girl of your choice, and bring her back here to the bus. You don't even have to ask her name. Call her honey and she'll be on her knees in seconds."

"You are a pig. I'd forgotten how much a pig you are. Didn't getting mono teach you anything?"

"Yes, not to kiss them. Who says you have to kiss the girls to have sex?"

Jack looked at his best friend with amazement. As much as he loved Axl, he would never understand how he could be so callous toward the other sex. Matt was different. During their time off, Matt became engaged to his girlfriend. Things had changed and even though she wasn't on tour with them, it was clear that the keyboardist of Dragon Slayers was on a very short leash.

"You get yourself someone, Axl. Don't worry about me. I'm fine."

"Are you still thinking about the tattoo girl?"

Jack winced. Although he hadn't spoken to her in three months, the pain from missing Molly still stung.

"I don't get it," Axl said as he fell into the leather chair facing Jack. "What makes her so special?"

"You wouldn't understand."

"Trust me. Maybe I will."

Jack shook his head and confessed, "She's it for me, Axl. She haunts my dreams. There's something about her that makes me know that I have to have her."

"Even though she can't look at your tats."

"We were working on that."

"Was it your idea or hers?"

"Both of ours."

"Are you sure?"

"What are you getting at?" Jack closed his laptop and looked at his friend with wary interest.

"You have a way of taking control and making everyone around you think it's a group decision. I'm wondering if she got swept up in whatever you were doing and finally had the chance to think about it once you left and realized it's not what she wants."

"I don't do that."

Axl laughed. "Man, that's how you've always operated. You're just lucky Ben and Matt don't complain."

"We're a band. The four of us have an equal say," Jack argued.

"We did have an equal say," Axl reminded him. "Then you decided that since you were the frontman for the band, you should make all of the decisions. Remember when we used to write our songs together? We'd hang out and just jam until we had music we were proud to play. Now, you come up with a song, and we all have to play along."

Axl leaned back in his seat, watching Jack with narrowed eyes. Axl loved writing music, but Jack had convinced him that his way was best for the group to succeed. The band deferred to him, trusting that his looks and talent would make them famous. Lately, it was bothering the guys that the accolades from the press were mostly for Jack Thomas, not Dragon Slayers.

"We've written music on this tour," Jack argued.

"Not much. Matt's written a few great songs while we've been off. He's worried you won't like them."

"Is this why you and the others think I'm going solo?"

"The thought did cross our minds," Axl admitted. "When you told us about your mom, we agreed to give you the benefit of the doubt."

"I've been with the three of you since we were kids. I'm not going to go solo now that we're finally making it."

"I wouldn't blame you if you did. You're getting all the attention now."

Jack ran his hand through his hair as he tried to process what Axl had told him.

"I knew there was something wrong. I never thought that I was the problem. I'm sorry."

"I wouldn't call you a problem," Axl said with a smirk. "You're more like a huge pain in the ass—talented, but still a pain in the ass."

"Looks like some things need to change then. I don't have to sing every song and I sure as hell don't have to write every song. And I damned well don't need to be the only one to answer questions at those stupid interviews. Your silence made me think you wanted me to run the band. Stand up to me when you don't agree with me. Your say is just as important as mine or Ben's or Matt's."

"I'm glad we got this sorted out. The others will be, too." Axl got to his feet. "About your tattoo girl," he said smiling, "how about forgetting about her for an hour or two. There's one hot chick hanging outside waiting to worship your rock star body. What do you say?"

"Go!" Jack ordered as he pointed to the bus door.

"Fine." Axl laughed. "You wouldn't know what to do with her any way."

Jack reached for his cell phone. He checked it for any sign that Molly had tried to reach him. He didn't know how someone could do that, cut themselves off completely from someone without an explanation. He'd sent her flowers and more presents, only to have them declined. It gnawed at his gut. His heart ached. He found himself rubbing his chest whenever he thought of Molly. He wondered if she ever thought of him or was he just another guitarist that got kicked to the curb.

Maybe Axl and Stevie were right. Maybe Jack was pushing Molly too hard to accept him. He was the one trying to convince her to look at his tattoos without being afraid. He was the one with rules insisting that he knew best. Tattoo dolls, storybooks, celibacy. What made him an expert? Molly probably felt relieved to have Jack leave her and give her time to realize that he was too much work.

Jack pulled up the tour schedule on his cell phone. One month to go and then he would have the chance to talk to Molly face-to-face. It was the only way he could try to explain things to her. If she still rejected him, then maybe the ache in his chest would go away.

twenty-two

Molly didn't visit her mother, Nancy, very often. Despite her love of rain, she didn't like Seattle's cold and dreary weather, and she didn't like her mother's husband. Molly refused to use the word stepfather because the man was nothing like a father to her. When he married Molly's mother, he made it very clear to Molly that he wasn't interested in being her father. He didn't like children. Molly wondered how her mother could marry a man who didn't like children and then realized that her mother would choose anyone over being alone.

Molly wasn't like that. Her history with men proved that she chose her own company over a man's every time. Jess was right. Molly would find any reason she could to leave a relationship. As much as she dreamed about having her happily ever after, she wouldn't take the next step toward it.

She heard the light tap on her bedroom door. "Come in."

Molly's mother opened the door just enough to give her a view of Molly. She peeked around the door and smiled. "Mind if I come in? I brought your favourites—Americano and a toasted sesame seed bagel with lots of butter."

Molly sat up in her bed, and smiled at her mother, giving her the invitation to join her.

"You had a long sleep. Sometimes the rain can do that to a person. I know when I first moved here all I wanted to do was curl up in my bed and sleep."

"I love the rain, Mom. I haven't been sleeping well for awhile. I guess everything's just caught up with me."

"Talk to me, sweetie. What's been going on with you?" She sat on the edge of the bed and handed Molly her coffee. "You know that you can tell me anything."

Molly sipped from the coffee cup as she thought about how to start the conversation. It wasn't easy telling her mother that she was pregnant, and the father wasn't in the picture.

"It's that rock star, isn't it?"

"His name is Jack, Mom."

Nancy folded her hands and placed them on her lap. "I saw a picture of him in one of the celebrity magazines. Did you know he is the son of Quinn Thomas?"

"Yes, Mom, I know that."

"His sister is a concert cellist. She's gay. Did you know that?"

Molly knew this routine all too well. Her mother wouldn't stop asking questions until Molly started talking.

"I met her girlfriend. She's beautiful."

"And gay."

Molly smiled. "I think they prefer the term lesbian, but yes, she's gay, too."

"Is Jack gay?"

"No, Mom. Jack's not gay. He's into women."

"Was he into you?"

"I thought so."

"So, what happened?"

"He had to leave."

"Why?"

"Mom!"

"He left. Why? Did you have a fight?"

"No, Mom. We didn't have a fight. He left a note for me to say he had to leave, and I haven't heard from him since."

"You haven't heard from him, or you haven't spoken to him?"

Molly took a bite of her bagel and stared at the floral pattern on her bedspread. Her mother knew how she handled breakups and how Molly avoided confrontations.

"I haven't spoken to him."

"Why?"

"Because I don't want to be lied to. I don't want to hear some lame excuse as to why he left a note on my pillow and took off. I deserve better than that."

"I see."

"What do you see?"

"That you're making excuses again. Molly, I love you, and I want what's best for you. You know that, don't you?"

"Yes."

"Honey, I try my best not to interfere with your love life, and I think I've done alright up to now, even though I told you to stay away from men with tattoos."

Molly nodded her head. "You've been good that way."

"Good, then you shouldn't mind me saying this. Molly, you need to see this relationship through to the end. You're ending it without giving him the benefit of the doubt. Find out why he left you. Was it another woman? Did he have a change of heart? Did he have a family emergency? Don't break up with him like you've done with every other man. Jack's been good for you. Don't give up so soon."

Molly looked at her mother, astonished at hearing her advice. "You've been talking with Jess, haven't you?"

"She called me. She wanted to make sure you arrived here safely."

"Jess could have called me."

"She calls me sometimes, too. We get along."

"I bet you do," Molly said with suspicion. "What else did she tell you?"

"Nothing. Only that Jack was helping you get past your fear of tattoos, something that none of the specialists could do for you. He cares for you, Molly. From what Jess told me, he's fallen quite hard for you."

"He left me, Mom," Molly said as she wiped away the tears.

"Call him, Molly. Talk to him."

"I love him."

"Tell him that."

"I'm pregnant."

"Well then, you have to tell him that, too."

twenty-three

Jess looked up from the bar and cursed. She hadn't expected him to show his face here again. After a few weeks of hoping he would ride in on his white horse or black Volkswagen Beetle, in this case, to reunite with Molly, she gave up on Jack Thomas, thoroughly disappointed.

"You're late," she said as she poured him a whiskey.

"It's a bit early isn't it to be serving alcohol?"

"No one else is here. Take it."

Jack took the offered glass and drank it in one gulp. "Thanks. Mind if I have another?"

"Looks like you've changed your taste in alcohol since you were last here. Probably applies to your taste in women, too." She poured his drink and one for herself. "Up yours."

"Thanks." Jack tossed back the drink and put the empty glass on the bar. "My taste in women has never changed. It's always been Molly."

"That's a laugh."

"It wasn't meant to be funny."

"If you're looking for her, you're in luck. She got back from Seattle last night."

"Who's in Seattle?"

"Someone."

"May I see Molly?"

"No. She's not here."

"Mind if I wait?"

"Suit yourself. She'll be gone for awhile."

"How long is awhile?"

"I don't know. How long does it take to make a phone call?"

"She wouldn't take my calls."

"You left her for Harley."

"I left with Harley to visit my mother in the hospital. She had an accident."

"You left with Harley."

"Who met up with my sister once my sister flew in from Europe. They are engaged, Jess. They are getting married. It's allowed in Canada."

"You didn't call."

"I left my phone in my car. I didn't know Molly's number and when I called here all I got was voicemail. She didn't return my calls."

"You could have explained yourself."

"I was in shock. I left a note telling her I would call her. I did. She didn't pick up."

"What took you so long?"

"Are we going to be playing twenty questions all morning?"

Jess stared at him.

"She changed her number. She returned my gifts. We went back on tour. I promised myself that I would come here as soon as we finished, and I would talk to her."

"Do you love her?"

"I never stopped. Does she love me?"

"You'll have to ask her yourself."

"That's why I'm here."

"Why don't you go for a coffee at a certain coffee shop and come back later."

"You could have told me that when I got here."

"Where would the fun be in that?"

Jack left Maguire's without saying another word to Jess. He cursed himself for not driving his car. He had to see Molly now, not in the twenty minutes it would take to walk to the coffee shop, and so he ran. He felt raindrops before he made it to the first intersection. This time, Jack had no leather jacket to protect him from the downpour. Within minutes, his long-sleeved white dress shirt was soaked. His tattoos became more visible as the fine cotton clung to his torso. There was no hiding them from her now. His jeans stuck to his legs. His boots made squishing sounds as they hit the payment with each stride.

Jack stopped when he made it to the entrance of the coffee shop. Seeing his disheveled reflection in the door's glass, he wiped his face with his hand, pushing his long hair out of his eyes, and then opened the door. His heart pounded. He'd never felt this way before—anxious yet excited to see Molly. Too much time had passed by giving her enough time to forget about him, to find someone new and move on with her life.

He hadn't moved on. Every day he thought of her. Every night she visited him in his dreams and promised to love him. Jack convinced himself that if they weren't meant to be, Molly would stop haunting his dreams.

Molly sat at her favourite table watching the rain pelt down. She sipped her decaf Americano coffee and remembered a time when perfection on two legs walked into this place and shared her table with her. He rocked her world and then left her. She could feel the burn in her cheeks as she imagined Jack with another woman. "I don't get jealous," she mumbled.

She closed her eyes, remembering the last night they spent together. Jack refused to make love to her, but his kisses and soft caresses brought her to orgasm more than once. He called her his angel. He promised to love her. He told her to trust him. Molly tried to call Jack several times. She'd find his number on her phone, and when his profile picture appeared, she would chicken out. She knew why. She was afraid, afraid to hear the words that he had found someone new, afraid to hear that he didn't love her. However, her biggest fear was that he'd discovered that she wasn't the right person for him. Just like she'd dumped boyfriends without a second thought, Molly was afraid that Jack had done the same to her. He had become tired of her stubbornness and silly rules and trying to get her to see his tattoos and given up on her.

I'm pregnant. Her hand went to her abdomen. She couldn't tell him; especially if he had found someone new. He deserved to be with someone who loved him unconditionally, someone who could look at him and love what she saw on the inside and the outside. Molly wouldn't tie him to her, not to a woman who couldn't give him what he needed. She felt a shiver run down her spine. She shook her head and took a deep breath. No more wasting time thinking about Jack. She had someone new to think about, someone she would love unconditionally.

"Is this seat taken?"

Molly opened her eyes and stared. His hair was longer than she remembered, and his face sported a few days' growth of beard, but his eyes were still the mesmerizing blue that had captured her heart.

"May I join you, Molly?"

"What are you doing here?"

"I heard this was the best place to get coffee. I bought you one." Jack held out a cup of coffee to her. "It's decaf. The server said it's your new drink of choice."

Molly took the offered cup and placed it on the table in front of her. "Thanks. Please sit." She couldn't stop looking at him. It wasn't fair that after all this time he had become sexier while she had become—

"Molly?"

"Umm?"

"I asked you how you are feeling. You look fantastic, almost glowing."

"I'm fine, Jack," she said as she pulled at the T-shirt clinging to her belly. "What brings you here?"

"You, of course."

"Why?"

"Why?"

"Yes, why are you here?"

"You wouldn't answer my calls or my texts. I don't know why you stopped all communication with me. We promised each other to make us work."

"You were the one who left me."

"I left you a note. My mother had an accident. She broke her leg and wrist and was in the hospital with a concussion. I had to go home."

"You could have woken me."

"Maybe I should have, but it was three o'clock in the morning. I wasn't thinking clearly. I had just enough sense to write you a note. I don't even remember driving to the airport."

"You were seen with Harley."

"She's my sister's fiancé." Jack reached for her hand and gently squeezed it, desperate for her to believe what he was telling her. "We travelled together to see my parents and Stevie."

"You could have called me."

"I tried, angel. You wouldn't take my calls."

Molly turned her attention to stare out the window.

Jack continued, "I called your cell phone, and I called Maguire's. I texted you. I sent you flowers, and you sent them back. When we went out on tour, I never stopped thinking about you. I counted the days for the tour to end so that I could get out here and talk to you face-to-face. You need to believe my story, Molly. I may have left you, but my heart never did."

"Stories are fiction, Jack. Don't you know that?"

"Not always. They can be real life fairy tales. They can have their happily ever after endings."

"Like your parents? We're not your parents, Jack. We are not love at first sight, and babies, and still in love twenty-five years later."

"Yes, we are. I know we are."

"Is that because you don't have a Plan B?"

"Yes, and because I love you. I've never stopped loving you."

"You don't know me, Jack."

"How can you say that?"

"Because it's true."

"Don't give me that crap. I know enough about you to know that I want to spend my life with you. You are passionate, stubborn, loving, extremely quick to judge, incorrectly I might add, and smart. You don't trust easily, and you're ready to fight for what you believe in even when you're wrong. I know where you love to be touched and how. You respond to me in a way you've never responded to another man. Do you know how I know that?"

"No."

"It's in the way you call my name when you climax. It's in the way you beg me to make love to you and when I don't you trust my reason why I don't. You trust me, Molly. You love me enough that you trust me to make us work."

"I've lost that trust."

"Then we'll get it back."

"How?"

"We'll date. Remember that we said we needed to date each other?"

"I think we're passed dating, Jack."

"Never. Couples should always date. It's the perfect way to stay connected."

"We're not a couple. Not now."

"We can be. Just give us a chance."

"So much has happened."

Molly turned her head and stared out the window.

"Who's in Seattle? Have you met someone, and he lives there? Is that why you don't want to give me a chance?"

Molly didn't answer him. Her gaze focused on the rain.

"Are you telling me you don't love me? Look at me, Molly. Tell me that you don't love me and that there's someone else. Tell me that and I'll leave you alone."

Molly turned to look at Jack with teary eyes. She kept her head up and held his gaze. "It won't work. We aren't going to have the happily ever after you so desperately want. It's over. Please accept that and leave me alone."

Jack released her hand as though it burned him. Her words stung, piercing his heart. "Axl was right. I took control of our relationship. You never wanted to be with me, not the way I wanted you. I just couldn't see it. You shouldn't have to work at trying to love me, and I shouldn't have to make you try. You either love all of me, or you don't love me at all. I'm sorry." Jack pushed to his feet and gazed at Molly one last time. "Goodbye, Molly. I hope you find your happily ever after."

Jack turned and exited the coffee shop. He didn't care that it was still raining outside. No one could tell that he was crying in the rain.

twenty-four

"So? Where is he?"

Molly ignored Jess's question, walking directly to her office. She locked the door behind her. It wasn't long before she heard Jess trying to open the door.

"Molly? Let me in. Don't shut me out. Did you see him? Did you see Jack? What happened?"

Molly continued to ignore Jess. She turned on her stereo, not caring what music played, and cranked up the volume. She didn't want to hear Jess's demands for answers. She didn't have any to give her, at least none that would make any sense to Jess. Molly looked at the leather couch. She wanted to throw herself on it and cry, but the memory of making love to Jack on that couch was too painful. Molly grabbed her dragon and lay down on the floor.

Jess went back to the bar and retrieved the spare keys for the office. She opened the door and found Molly in the fetal position on the floor.

"Molly!" Jess ran to Molly and knelt beside her. She pulled the dragon away from Molly's face. "What are you doing on the floor?"

"This was the only place I could lie down without being reminded of Jack."

Jess got up and turned off the stereo. She turned to face Molly, crossing her arms over her chest. "What did he say?"

"He explained everything."

"And?"

"He told me he loved me and that we belonged together."

"And?"

"I told him that we didn't have a happily ever after in our story, and then I asked him to leave."

"You did what?"

"You heard me."

"Did you tell him about the baby?"

"No."

"Why in heaven's name didn't you tell him?"

"Because I was too afraid to." Molly covered her face with her hands and sobbed.

"Afraid of what?"

"Not being the person he thinks I am. It's better for him to leave me now than later."

"For crying out loud, Molly. The man has been in love with you since the day he met you. He knows you're crazy. He's put up with all the crap you've thrown at him, and yet he still comes back for more. What makes you think he'll leave you?"

"I'd leave me. I'm a terrible girlfriend, remember? He'd stay with me for awhile and then get tired of me and leave. You know it's true."

"That's not true. You should have told Jack the truth. He has a right to know."

"Leave me alone!"

"You've done some crazy things, Molly Maguire, but this tops them all. I just don't understand you."

Jess left Molly in her office. After telling the staff not to bother Molly under any circumstances, she donned her raincoat and left to find Jack. A quick call to the reservations desk of the only hotel in Ingledale let her know that Jack was a registered guest. A promise of free drinks at Maguire's gave her Jack's room number.

It took several minutes of knocking on Jack's door for Jess to succeed in getting Jack to answer it. Freshly showered and shaved with only a towel wrapped around his waist, Jack's tattoos took Jess by surprise. Her eyes opened wide as she drank in the vivid pictures inked so beautifully on his skin. For a brief moment, she pitied Molly for not seeing them for herself.

"Jess." There was no hiding the disappointment in his voice.

"May I come in?"

"Sure." Jack opened the door wide and gestured for her to enter his suite. "You caught me while I was in the shower. Let me get dressed and I'll be right with you."

"Sorry to bother you."

"No bother," Jack said as he rummaged through his suitcase and pulled out clothing to wear.

Jess watched in amazement as Jack dropped his towel and pulled on his jeans and then a T-shirt.

"What can I do for you," he asked as he tucked his shirt into his jeans.

"I spoke with Molly."

"So did I. She told me she didn't love me. She asked me to leave. You could have told me as much when I spoke with you at the bar."

"I didn't know she was going to tell you that. She's not thinking properly. Please don't give up on her."

"She's the one who has given up, Jess. Tell me, is it true she has someone in Seattle? I don't blame her if she has, although I would have appreciated a call or text."

"Her mother lives in Seattle."

"Her mother?"

"Yes. Molly wasn't feeling well, so she stayed with her mother for a few days."

"Molly looked great when I saw her. She was glowing."

"Well, I guess the Seattle air has great medicinal properties."

He took two bottles of beer out of the bar fridge and offered one to Jess. "So, has she?"

Jess took the offered beer. "Found someone else? No."

"I guess that's some consolation." Jack offered Jess a seat on the couch, and then sat beside her. "What can I do for you? Did you come here to say goodbye?"

"No. I came here to tell you to stay."

"And do what exactly?"

"Convince her that she's wrong. Convince her that she won't be a disappointment to you."

"Whatever gave her that idea? I have never said anything to her to make her think that."

"She thinks she's too much work for you and that you'll eventually give up on her."

"That's not true. Everything I have done for her proves that I won't give up on her."

"Tell her that."

"What can I say to her that I haven't already? She's the most head-strong person I know. Molly's always right even when she's wrong. That's what she told me, and she made me agree to that. There's no arguing with her."

"Yes, but now she's bat shit crazy wrong, and I think she'll admit to it."

"Jess—"

"She's pregnant."

Jack took a long drink from his beer. He heard Jess say something about the pill and antibiotics and loss of effectiveness and that the baby was his.

"Jack? Did you hear what I said? Molly's pregnant with your baby."

"Why didn't she tell me?"

"Because since you went away, she has been living in one very long blonde moment. She hasn't been thinking straight where you are concerned. That's why you have to go to her."

XO XO XO

Jack found Molly on her office floor, cuddling the stuffed dragon. By the sound of her soft snores, he could tell that she was sleeping. He smiled at his angel whose blonde hair fanned out messily around her, framing the beautiful face that haunted his dreams. Jack knelt beside her and kissed her forehead. "You are the most stubborn woman I have ever known," he said with admiration.

Jack carefully slid his arms under her body. He lifted her with ease and laid her gently on the leather couch. Molly grumbled something unintelligible and hugged her dragon tighter. She quietened once Jack covered her with the throw blanket he retrieved from the back of the couch. Then he sat on the floor beside her, leaned against the couch and waited.

He felt the light touch of her fingers as she played with his hair. Her fingers caressed the long strands working their way up to his scalp and then slowly working their way back down to his shoulders. Jack relaxed against her touch, giving her access to more of him if she wanted.

"Your hair has grown," she murmured.

"Do you like it, or should I get it cut?"

"I kind of like it like this."

"I'll keep it long for you then."

They remained silent for the longest moment. Molly continued to play with Jack's hair while he sat quietly enjoying the attention he had missed over the past few months. Jack decided to let Molly take the lead in what happened next.

"I'm not her, you know. I can never be her."

"Who can't you be?"

"I can't be your mother. You'll get tired of me, and then you'll leave."

Jack turned to face Molly. His gaze searched her face for a clue as to what she was thinking. "I don't want you to be my mother. I never have. What makes you think that?"

"She's the woman of your dreams, your stories, your tattoos. You did all of that for her so that you could be her knight in shining armour. You've put your mother's stories on your body, Jack. There's no room for me."

"Is that what you think?"

"You told me so yourself. You got tattoos to show your mother you'd be by her side while she fought cancer. They're a tribute to her. I get it now."

"You are wrong."

"I'm never wrong."

Jack stood up and looked down at Molly, his eyes darkening with emotion. His fingers went to his shirt buttons. He unbuttoned his shirt slowly, making the buttons pop with the sound he knew turned Molly on.

"What are you doing?" Molly asked as she sat up, still clinging to the dragon.

"I'm proving you wrong, angel."

"I can't look."

"Yes, you can, and you will. You owe me that much."

Molly squeezed her eyes shut. She heard Jack's shirt drop to the floor.

"Open your eyes, Molly. Trust me. Please. Open your eyes."

"Show me Finley first. I can look at Finley."

Jack smiled as he turned around. "Okay, look at Finley."

Jack knew she had opened her eyes when he heard her gasp. He waited for her to say something. She stood instead, touching him with her fingers, slowly tracing each scale of the dragon's blue-green skin and each spike of his spine. Jack undid his belt and pulled his pants down past his hips. His shoulders dropped as he relaxed under her touch. He closed his eyes and focused on remembering this moment for the rest of his life.

Molly touched the tip of the dragon's tail that started at the top of Jack's right hip and wound across to his left then up into its body. The dragon's hind feet dug into Jack's rib cage. Each talon bloodied where it dug into Jack's flesh. The effect was spectacular. The dragon's body covered Jack's back, its magnificent wingspan spread from the left lower rib to the right shoulder.

"Harley did this?"

"Yes."

"Finley looks as though he could fly away with you."

"Sometimes I dream that he does."

Molly touched the dragon's neck from the middle of Jack's upper back to his left shoulder leading to Jack's torso. Her fingers made their way down his shoulder to the side of his arm where the dragon's left front foot dug into Jack.

"Does he scare you?"

"No."

"Why?"

"Because he's beautiful." Molly kissed Jack's back and then once again trailed her fingers over the dragon's scales and spine. "I like the blood on his talons."

"You do?"

"Yes. It's very realistic. You don't have a tattoo of a dragon on your back. You have a dragon on your back. There's a big difference."

"You should tell that to Harley."

"Don't push it."

"Are you ready to see my chest?"

"Give me a second. I'm still admiring Finley."

"Take your time, love. There's no rush."

Jack waited patiently. This wasn't how he had planned it. Molly was supposed to finish drawing on the tattoo doll. She was supposed to prepare herself for what she would see. He hoped they weren't making a big mistake. It was too late to stop now.

"I'm ready," her voice was strong and confident.

"Are you sure?"

"Turn around, Jack. It's time to see Finley's head and whatever else you have on your chest."

Jack turned around slowly. He focused on Molly's face, watching every twitch, every movement of her eyes, and the quiver of her lips.

Molly forced herself to look at the dragon's head. She knew the head and found comfort in knowing that it wouldn't scare her. "He's biting you!" Molly's hand pressed against Jack's chest over his heart. "Why is he doing this?" She looked up at Jack's face with concern. "It's not in your mother's stories. Why did you do this, Jack?"

Jack put his hand over Molly's. "It's okay. Trust me. He's fighting me, but I'm fighting him, too. Take your hand away. Look at my story, Molly. Take a good look at it."

Jack released her hand and waited for Molly to remove hers. She took her hand away and stared at the dragon's head. There was no denying he was beautiful. His mouth opened wide, his long, sharp fangs biting into Jack's chest over his heart. His teeth were red with Jack's blood. His nostrils flared, and his eyes were wild with rage or was it fear?

Molly's gaze moved to Jack's left arm. He told her it was their family vine, belonging only to them and their children. She had seen the lower part of it, and now she could see it in its full beauty. The black and grey vine that wound its way up Jack's arm had only one rose, Molly's rose. The vine was thorny and at the top of the vine was the dragon's foot, pierced by the vine's thorns. Blood dripped from its wound. Molly reached out and touched the wound, almost feeling sorry for its injury.

"Look down," Jack said softly, encouraging her to be brave.

Her gaze left the dragon's wound, looked past his teeth tearing into Jack's chest and found the black knight, the dragon slayer with his sword thrust toward the dragon's throat. In the other hand, he held a shield with the letter T for Thomas emblazoned on it. Underneath the knight was his majestic black steed, who stood on his powerful hind legs, rearing upwards toward the dragon, hooves pawing at the air, eager for battle.

Molly's fingers touched the horse's long and wild mane. "He's beautiful. Does he have a name?"

"Goliath."

"Hello, Goliath. You are a beautiful boy."

"What else do you see, love?"

Molly looked closer at the dragon slayer's face. She knew that face. She recognized the chiseled jaw line, the mouth with lips formed in fierce determination, and the piercing blue eyes that reflected the dragon's fire. "You're the knight. That's not much of a surprise, Jack."

"Look again."

"The background is your castle. I like the shades of grey. It's very subtle and the perfect background for your knight."

"I'm glad you approve. What else do you see?"

Molly's gaze went to his right arm. It was identical to his left arm yet filled with roses. Each rose displayed the name of a family member. "Everyone's on this arm?" she asked as she touched Stevie's name and Cat's.

"Everyone. There's room for more if and when David and Stevie have children. There's more, Molly. I can't believe that you don't see it. Keep looking."

"On your chest?"

"Yes."

Molly returned her gaze to Jack's chest. She started at the dragon's head and moved her gaze slowly down his torso. She listed off each tattoo as she found it, "Dragon's head. Bite marks. Knight's sword. Knight's shield with crest. Castle. Flag on the castle. Goliath. Goliath's mane. Goliath's feathery legs. Knight's legs in stirrups. A woman's legs behind his." Molly went quiet. She didn't know how she had overlooked the woman sitting behind the knight on the horse. Her gown billowed out behind her as she wrapped her arms around the knight's waist and clung to his back. The shading was perfect, giving the knight's ladylove long blonde hair that framed her face, a face with full lips and pale blue-grey eyes.

"That's me."

"Yes."

"When did you put me there?"

"You've always been there. I swear it. I've only added your rose since I met you."

"How did you know?" Molly's voice was barely a whisper.

"What you looked like?"

"Yes."

"You've haunted my dreams for as long as I can remember. There was no forgetting your face if I tried."

"Haunted? That doesn't sound good."

"You haunted me by tempting me with your kisses, touching me with your soft hands and promising more, only to leave me before morning."

"I'm sorry."

"Don't be. I loved dreaming of you. I still do. That's what happens when you're in love."

Molly hugged Jack's waist. He kissed the top of her head while caressing her hair.

"I want to love you. I do love you. It's just that this has happened all so fast."

"I know. There's no rush. We have all the time in the world to fall in love and to stay in love." Jack stepped back and took Molly by the hand. He sat on the couch and pulled her onto his lap. "You are right about my tattoos. My mother's stories inspired them. When I was young, I pretended I was a world-famous musician or a medieval knight. I wasn't the only one. Stevie and David played the same make-believe games with me. Stevie would be the female dragon slayer or the magical cellist whose music saved the world. David preferred to save the world with his soccer kick, but then he is four years younger than we are.

"When Mom got sick, I wanted so much to be that knight who would kick cancer's ass out of our lives and make Mom well again. The only way I knew how to do this was to take the dragon on myself and so I asked Harley to help me. I was away at university, making it easy for me to stay away from Mom until the tattoos were finished. I worked part time as a bartender to help pay for them. I knew Mom would be pissed if she thought my university money went into these."

"What about your dad?"

"He was shocked at first. Then he told me to remember that my mom loved me, and she'd get over the initial shock when she saw these for the first time. He was right. My dad knew my mom's reaction down to every last word."

"I'm the world's worst girlfriend."

"Does this mean we're back together?"

"Yes."

Jack laughed. "You're not the world's worst girlfriend. I haven't known enough women to know if that's true or not."

"That isn't funny."

"I'm allowed to make a joke. It's not a blonde joke. I remember your rules."

"I'm still the worst girlfriend."

"Why? Because you wouldn't look at my tattoos?"

"Yes, and because . . ."

"Because what?"

"You don't know everything about me."

"I know everything about you, Molly Maguire."

"Not everything."

"I know about the baby. You should have told me."

Molly looked at him with wonder in her eyes.

"I'm here because I love you. The baby is a bonus."

"It wasn't in your Plan A or your Plan B. Admit it, Jack."

"You are my plan everything, Molly. A baby fits in perfectly. What do you think of the name Prince or Princess tattooed right here above yours?"

twenty-five

"This feels silly," Molly said when she heard the knock on her office door.

"Let him do this. Don't be a spoilsport," Jess admonished her. "Besides, how many girls have gone on a date with Jack Thomas?"

Molly opened her office door to find Jack standing with a bouquet of red roses and a box of chocolate covered almonds. "The roses are for you and the chocolates are for Jess. I heard you didn't share the last box that I sent you."

Molly turned and stuck out her tongue at Jess. "It seems like Jess likes to talk about me behind my back."

"I'm allowed. Besides, if I didn't, you two wouldn't be standing here, would you?" she said as she made her way to Jack and took the presents.

"She's got a point," Jack agreed.

"So where are you two love birds off to?"

"The movies," Jack answered. "There's a movie in town I want Molly to see."

"Will you be home late?" Jess teased. "Molly has a curfew now that she's in the family way."

Jack laughed while Molly groaned her response. "Don't worry. We'll be back in time for my first set."

"Say goodbye, Jess," Molly said tersely.

"Goodbye and have fun."

"Sometimes I could strangle her," Molly said as Jack escorted her out of the bar.

"She's doing what best friends do. Axl, Ben, Matt and I tease each other constantly. Do you think we can walk, or would you like me to drive?"

"The theatre is only two blocks west of here, Jack. I think I can make it."

"Good. Then I can hold your hand longer." Jack took her hand as they started to walk to their destination.

"What movie are we seeing? I didn't know there are matinees at this time."

"You'll find out when we get there. Trust me. You'll like it." Jack gazed down at Molly and smiled. "How are you feeling today?"

"Better today. I'm glad the morning sickness has stopped. Three months was a bit much if you ask me. Don't forget my scan is on Monday."

"I'm looking forward to it. Do you think we'll find out the baby's sex?"

"I don't know, but I want it to be a surprise. Do you mind?"

"No. I like surprises. I like giving them, too."

"Oh, I know you do, dragon slayer. I'd say this little bundle proves it."

Jack stopped and pulled Molly to face him. There was no mistaking the love that twinkled in his eyes, instantly making her feel weak at the knees. "It took two of us to make that surprise, love, don't you remember?"

"I do remember. I'm just wondering if it was our first time or second."

Jack looked up at the sky as though he would find the answer there. "First time works for me," he said looking back at her.

"Why the first time?"

"Because I knew that night that I loved you."

Molly felt tears start to form. She wiped at them with the back of her hand. "Damned hormones."

"Come on. We don't want to be late for the movie."

Molly couldn't believe her eyes when she saw the theatre marquis. "*The Basset Hound Detective?* You've got to be kidding me."

"You said it was one of your favourite movies. It's one of mine, too."

Jack paid for their tickets, and then escorted Molly into the theatre's lobby. "Popcorn?"

"Yes, please and a root beer."

Jack gave the server his order, "We'll have two large popcorns and two root beers."

"This place is empty, Jack. Are you sure the movie's playing?"

"They wouldn't have sold us tickets or popcorn if the movie wasn't playing."

"It's an old movie. Maybe that's why no one is here to see it."

"Or maybe everyone is already in the theatre, and we're the last to arrive."

"I didn't think of that."

Jack gave Molly a knowing look.

"Don't you dare say it."

"The thought never crossed my mind." Jack handed Molly her bag of popcorn and drink, and then nodded toward the entrance to the theatre. "This way. The movie is about to start."

Molly stopped when she saw the empty seats.

"Surprise," he whispered in her ear.

"What have you done?"

"We needed to have our first movie date, and I thought this one suited us perfectly. What do you think?"

"You're right. It is perfect."

"Go ahead. Pick our seats."

Molly picked seats that were dead centre. Once she settled in her seat, Jack took his seat beside her.

"I can't believe you did this."

"Anything for you. You know that."

The lights dimmed, and the movie started. Molly held Jack's hand and didn't let go. Jack marvelled at how expertly she could manage her drink and eat popcorn with one hand. He wished he could do the same. When Molly saw him try to balance his bag of popcorn on his lap, she chuckled and offered him hers.

"You haven't done this before, have you?"

"I have, but since you won't let go of my hand, it's somewhat difficult."

"You've never held hands with a girl at the movies?"

Jack gazed over at her. "I have, but she would always let go."

"Not a chance, dragon slayer. You're mine.

XO XO XO

They were still holding hands when they left the theatre.

"I forgot how much fun that movie is," Molly said happily.

"I'm glad you liked it. We watch it every once in awhile when we want to bug my dad."

"Care to elaborate?"

"Dad hates to watch his movies. He'll only watch them if Mom asks him to, or when it's our turn to pick a family movie night, and we choose one of his films. He's not allowed to say no."

"Any of his movies?"

"Not the ones with lots of sex in it. That's just too weird."

"I can imagine it is." Molly noticed that they weren't walking back toward Maguire's. "Where are you taking me now?"

"Can you manage a couple more blocks?"

"I think so."

"Good."

"We're heading out of the business section of town, Jack. There are only houses this way."

"Then we're not lost."

"I don't know about that. How's your sense of direction?"

"I found you, didn't I?"

"Oh please. That line is so corny."

"Get used to it, love. I've been saving them all for you."

Molly laughed. She let go of Jack's hand and put her arm around his waist and pressed against his side. He kissed the top of her head.

"I know this area. I haven't been here in years, but it looks the same."

"Is that good or bad?"

"It's good. Are you taking me to where I think you're taking me?"

"I don't know. Am I?"

"I used to play in that park," Molly said, pointing to an open area with swings and slides. "Dad would take me there when he had some time off."

"Do you want to stop?"

"No. Let's keep walking."

Jack could feel Molly's excitement as her steps quickened and her fingernails dug into his waist. He let her pull him along the sidewalk until she stopped suddenly. He held her close as they both gazed at her family home.

"I've been avoiding coming here. Once my mother sold the house, I didn't want to look at it again. All the memories—"

"Do you want to leave?"

"No! I'm glad you brought me here. Now you can see part of my story."

The house was built in the sixties, two-stories with gray siding and white trim. A white picket fence enclosed the lush green yard littered with toys. A swinging loveseat hung on the front porch. Everything about the house made it a home.

"That was my bedroom up there, the second window from the left. It's a three-bedroom house. Two bathrooms and a big kitchen. At least that's what it had. It's been years since I last saw the inside so it may have changed."

"What about the backyard?"

"Huge. At least, when you're little, everything looks huge."

"Do you want to go and take a look?"

"What? No. I couldn't. Right here is as close as I want to be."

"Tell me. Are your memories of this place happy or sad?"

"All happy, Jack. Even when my dad died, I found comfort here. It just wasn't the same when Mom remarried. It didn't feel right to live in the house without Daddy." Molly looked up at Jack. "Do you mind if we head back? I'm feeling tired."

"Let's go."

"Head this way," Molly said as she pointed down the street. "I know a shortcut."

XO XO XO

"So, how did your first date go?" Jess asked them when they returned to Maguire's.

"The best," Molly answered as she hurried to the office.

"She has to pee," Jack announced.

"Thanks for sharing." Jess offered Jack a beer. "How was the movie?"

"Just as much fun as I remembered. Molly loved it, too. We went for a walk afterwards. I took her to her old house."

"How did she react?"

"She loved the surprise. It's a beautiful house."

"It is, isn't it? Perfect for raising a family."

twenty-six

Molly squeezed Jack's hand in a futile attempt to calm his nerves. "Jack, if you can't sit still, you'll have to leave. You're upsetting the baby."

"How can I be upsetting the baby? I'm tapping my foot."

"Well, your foot tapping is sending vibrations through me and right into the baby. Stop it."

"Sorry."

Jack stood up from the uncomfortable plastic chair in the ultrasound room. He looked at the various posters stuck to the wall painted in typical hospital green showing various stages of a baby's development during gestation. He pointed to where their baby should be. "That's our little one."

"Let's take a look and see, shall we?" the technician asked as she prepared Molly's round tummy for the scan. "I've warmed up the gel. No one likes to get that cold shock when they have a full bladder."

Molly smiled her appreciation.

"Is this your first?"

"Yes," Jack answered. He took hold of Molly's hand and squeezed it gently.

"Can't you tell?" Molly asked her. "He hasn't settled since we got here."

"Well, not to worry, this won't take long. What we're looking for is normal development of the fetus. We can also date the pregnancy, and we can see if this is a multiple pregnancy."

"Multiple pregnancy?"

"Twins, Jack. That's what you and Stevie were."

"I know that. It's just that it never occurred to me that you could have twins."

"I doubt it. I don't have twins in my family."

"It doesn't always work that way," the technician said happily. "Sometimes twins just happen."

Jack and Molly watched in silence as the technician scanned Molly's abdomen. She pressed the wand against Molly's belly, typed on the keyboard, and then moved the wand to another spot. She repeated this several times, her gaze never leaving the machine's screen. The technician's silence was discomforting. Molly squeezed Jack's hand for support.

"Sorry for the delay. I had to make sure," the technician said. "Congratulations, Mom and Dad. You are having twins." She turned the screen to allow Molly and Jack to see the full view. "You can see them as clear as day and they look absolutely fine."

"Twins?" Molly asked, her mouth fell open as her eyes opened wide.

"Twins," Jack said, bursting with pride.

"I hate you, Jack Thomas."

"But you'll love them more."

XO XO XO

Molly stared at the ultrasound photograph she held in her hands. She hadn't spoken one word to Jack once they got into the car and headed back to Maguire's.

Jack, desperate to know what Molly was thinking, blurted out the first thing that came to mind, "Dads don't cause twins, Molly. It's what your eggs decided to do."

"You got me pregnant. You're to blame. It was your virgin sperm."

"What?" Jack sputtered, taking his focus off the road to look at her. "You don't honestly believe that."

Molly smiled at him, her eyes bright and filled with love. "Way to go, dragon slayer, anything to get that left arm of yours filled with roses."

"You're not mad?"

"I'm not mad, I'm scared shitless, Jack! I don't know anything about babies, and now I'm expecting two!"

Jack reached for Molly's hand and brought it to his lips. He kissed the palm of her hand and held it against his cheek. "We'll get through this, angel. Trust me."

XO XO XO

"How is she?" Jess asked once Jack joined her at the bar.

"She's sleeping."

"You have to admit, being told you're having twins is quite a shock."

"Tell me about it."

"Have you called your parents?"

"I will. I'm trying to deal with the news myself."

Jess handed Jack a glass of one of Maguire's best and most expensive single malt scotch. "This calls for only the best. Cheers."

"Cheers," Jack replied. He took a sip of his drink and smiled appreciatively.

"Can you imagine two little ones running around here? They'll be the cutest kids. You're sure she's having a boy and a girl?"

"When Molly heard twins, she wanted to know their sex. One has a penis, and the other doesn't."

He drank from his glass and looked at the pictures on the wall. They were all of Molly's family, most of them taken at Maguire's. Jack turned on his stool and stared at the booth where Molly played when she saw her father's murder. He could picture her as a little girl and see the horror on her face. He closed his eyes to block out the image. It was time for a change.

"Jack, what is it? What's wrong?"

He turned to face Jess. "Nothing's wrong. I was thinking about finding a new wall for some family pictures."

twenty-seven

"Close your eyes," Jack ordered Molly once she fastened her seatbelt.

She laughed when she felt him put a blindfold on her. "What kind of date have you planned today, Jack?"

"It's a surprise," he answered as he started the ignition, and then began to drive.

"They've all been surprises," she remarked. "I don't think I can take any more."

"You don't like my surprises?"

"I do, but sometimes you go a bit overboard."

"When have I ever gone overboard?"

"When? Let me think. How about when you rented Crosby's so that we could have the restaurant all to ourselves?"

"We're surrounded by people all day. I thought it would be good for us to have a place to ourselves."

"How about when you rented the auditorium so that you could give me my very own concert?"

"Didn't you like your birthday present?"

"I loved it, but that's not the point."

"We've had regular dates, too."

"Oh, I know, and I loved those, too. We could do more of them. I like going to the movies. I like walking the boulevard with you. We can even go out for coffee."

"Decaf coffee."

"Decaf coffee," she agreed.

"We will still do those. Just let me do this last one. Please."

"Fine."

"No more argument?"

"Will it do me any good?"

"Not in the least."

"That's what I thought. Where are we going?"

"Can't you tell?"

"You're taking too many turns for Ingledale. You're trying to mess with my sense of direction."

"You are good."

"Thanks."

Molly felt the Beetle slow down to a stop. She heard Jack engage the parking brake and then kill the engine. When she heard him release his seatbelt, her hands went to undo hers.

"Wait," he commanded.

"For what?"

"I have to make sure everything is in place. Promise me you won't peek."

"I promise."

Molly heard the driver's door open then shut. She was tempted to pull the blindfold off, but Jack's surprises were too good to spoil. She held her breath, straining to hear any sound that may be outside. She heard nothing. No cars. No birds. Nothing that would give her a clue. She startled when Jack opened her door.

"Are you ready?"

"Yes."

"Give me your hand."

Molly obeyed, holding her hand up to Jack. He took her hand and helped her out of the car. She could tell that there was grass beneath the soles of her shoes.

"You've taken me to a park."

"Not quite."

"You've bought me a pony. We're at a horse farm."

"You never told me you wanted a pony. Should I add that to the list?'

"No! Please. No pony."

"Not even for the kids?"

"Not even for the kids."

"Okay. For now." Jack put his arm around Molly's waist to guide her as they walked. "Put your hands out."

Molly touched wood, noting its painted surface. Her hands explored the wood and found points that had been made blunt. She felt the latch. It was a gate. "Jack, you didn't!" Molly pulled off her blindfold. She squinted against the afternoon sun, forcing her eyes to adjust to the light. "It's my house."

"It's our home now, Molly. We need a place to raise our babies and call home."

"How did you manage to buy this?"

"It doesn't matter."

"Jack. Tell me."

"Let's just say that I offered a price the owner found easy to accept. Very happily, too, I might add. Do you want to see it?"

"Of course, I do."

Jack opened the gate for Molly. She made her way up the walkway, taking her time so that she could she take in every detail of the house. Suddenly, she heard barking, a low bark that she remembered hearing not too long ago. She stopped and faced the direction from which it was coming.

"We have a dog? The house comes with a basset hound?"

Jack squatted down and called out to the dog, "Come here, Arnold. Come here, boy."

"His name is Arnold?"

"That's what his previous owners called him. I think it suits him, what do you think?"

The dog trotted up to Jack, wagging its tail excitedly. Jack petted him while cooing words of affection to him. "Who's the good dog? You are, Arnold, You're the good dog."

Molly held her hand out to him, unable to bend much at the waist. "Hi, Arnold. You're a pretty dog." She smiled when he licked her hand. "You didn't steal him, did you?"

Jack stood up to face Molly. "No! I saw an ad in the paper. His owners were moving in with their daughter somewhere in San Francisco, and they couldn't take him with them. It was perfect timing. We saw the *Basset Hound Detective* movie on our date, and I remembered that you loved this breed of dog. You told me shortly after I met you how much you wanted one when you were a little girl."

"We won't be able to look after a dog, Jack. Not with the twins coming so soon."

"We have a fenced in yard, one that I am told he cannot escape from unless we don't close this gate. He's four years old, completely housebroken, and as long as he is fed and watered, and has his favourite toy, he won't be any trouble."

Molly opened her mouth to speak.

"He'll be my responsibility until you've fallen completely in love with him and want to look after him yourself. I promise."

"Okay. We'll keep him."

"Hear that, Arnold? She likes you!" Jack kissed Molly's forehead. "Thank you. I don't know what I would have done if you said you didn't want him."

"May I see my house now?"

"I was wondering when you'd want to see it."

They walked to the front door with Arnold trotting happily beside them.

Jack opened the door for her. "Go ahead. It's our home, Molly."

She hesitated. Right away, she could see that the house wasn't what she remembered.

"It was a mess— pretty on the outside but ugly on the inside. I hope you like the changes I've made."

"You did all this?"

"With help. Lots of help."

"Do you mind if I take the tour by myself?"

"Are you sure?"

"I feel a big cry coming on, and I'd like to be alone. Don't worry. It's a good cry."

"Do you want Arnold to go with you? He knows every room. He could give you the tour."

"Yes. Arnold can come. I'd like that."

Jack pointed to the porch swing. "I'll be right here. Waiting. Patiently."

"Thanks. You can write a song about Arnold."

Molly kissed his cheek and then closed the door behind her.

Jack didn't write a song. He waited. He checked his watch many times. Ten minutes turned into twenty minutes that turned into thirty minutes. How long did it take to tour a house?

Jack opened the door and called out, "Molly!"

Only a single low woof from Arnold answered him. Instant panic grabbed at his insides as Jack ran up the stairs, heading to the master bedroom. He checked the bathroom. She wasn't there.

"Molly!" he called out as he turned and ran to the nursery.

Jack stopped in the doorway, almost afraid to disturb the scene before him. Molly cradled a stuffed animal in her arms while she rocked in the oversized rocking chair. Arnold sat at her feet wagging his tail. Jack leaned against the doorframe, waiting for his heart to stop pounding and for Molly to acknowledge him.

She didn't look at Jack when she spoke, "We have dragons in our babies' room."

"Not just dragons. I'm sure I saw a couple of teddy bears somewhere, pink and blue, and there's a cow, too."

"But mostly dragons."

"Finley and Fiona dragons, to be exact."

Molly pointed to the mural on the wall. "You've turned the nursery into *Jack and Stevie's Bedtime Stories.*"

"I see it as little Molly and Jack junior's room."

"We're not calling them that, Jack."

"Until we decide on names, it will have to do."

Jack moved toward her, wondering what she was thinking. Her reaction to the nursery hadn't been what he had expected. He didn't expect her to scare the hell out of him for starters, and he sure as hell didn't expect her to be this quiet.

Jack knelt down in front of her and took her hand. "If you hate it, I'll call the painters and have this room redone by tomorrow."

"I don't hate it, Jack. I love it."

"You love it?"

She gazed down at him with bright eyes. "This is our story, Jack. It's not your parents' story, and it's not yours and Stevie's. This is all ours. You're not fighting the dragon. You're playing with the dragon. He's happy, and so are you."

"All because of you."

"That's me standing in a rose garden."

"The resemblance is remarkable, isn't it?"

"How many kids do you expect me to have?" She looked down at him with narrowed eyes. "I'm not that kind of blonde, Jack. I know what it means."

"Did I ever say you were?"

"I'm just reminding you in case you forgot."

"Did you see the leather couch downstairs? I tried it out. It's perfect for taking naps. Just in case." There it was, that mischievous smile that took hold of her heart and never let go.

"I don't want you to sleep on that couch, Jack. As a matter of fact, I have other plans for you."

"What kind of plans?"

"I love the bed in the master bedroom. I'd like you to mess it up with me."

"How messy do you want to make it?"

"Why don't you come with me, and I'll show you." Molly held out her hand to Jack. He took hold of it and helped her get to her feet.

"Stay here, Arnold," Jack said with as stern a voice as he could muster.

Arnold didn't move a muscle.

"We haven't messed up a bed in awhile," Jack said as he followed her into the bedroom. "Not that I'm complaining."

"That's good to know." Molly sat on the edge of the bed. "Do you remember when you stripped off your clothes, and I couldn't watch you?"

"Yes. Why?"

"I'd like you to strip for me. This time, I want to watch."

Jack smiled. "You just want me to strip? Nothing else?"

"It all depends on how well you strip."

"Is that a challenge, my ladylove?"

"Are you up to it, dragon slayer?"

"What do I get in return?"

"I'm sure you'll think of something."

Molly made herself comfortable on the bed, leaning against the overstuffed pillows in front of the carved mahogany headboard. She saw it at once, the sparkle in his eyes that promised her everything and more, telling her that he had already won.

Jack toed off his canvas loafers, unbuckled his belt and pulled it out through the belt loops with a slow and deliberate motion. He dropped it to the floor. Not once did his gaze leave Molly's face. "Shirt or pants next?"

"Shirt. Please."

Jack took hold of the hem of his T-shirt then pulled it over his head. He waited for her instructions, very much aware that she was ogling his torso. He flexed his pectorals for fun.

Molly smiled appreciatively. "I like a rock star who keeps fit. If I don't like his music, at least I can admire his body."

"A backhanded compliment. Someone's feeling pretty cocky right now. I wonder why?" Jack mused. "Should I blame it on the hormones?"

"Blame everything on the hormones."

"For how long?"

"Forever. How's that?" Molly gestured with her hand for Jack to turn around. "I'd like to see my dragon please."

"When did he become yours?" Jack asked as he turned around.

"Ever since he came to me in my dreams." She could see his back straighten when he heard her words. "Jack?"

He turned to face her, fighting back tears. "You've dreamed of him?"

Molly nodded her head. "He's only visited me lately. And I only have good dreams about him. Finley doesn't hurt me. He's not hurting anyone. He's just there watching over us. Watching over our babies."

Jack rushed to Molly and took her in his arms. He held her for the longest moment.

"Do you remember telling me that your tattoos were pictures of your family, a tribute to everyone you loved?"

"Yes."

"I think that Finley is what brought us together. I feel it deep inside me. If it weren't for your tattoos, I'm sure we would have had our one-night stand, and that would have been it for us. You would have been my rock star fantasy who left in the morning, and nothing would have changed in my life."

"You still might have gotten pregnant."

"I'm trying to be serious here." Molly pushed away from Jack so that she could look into his eyes and make him understand. "It's because you wanted me to see these," she said as she ran her hands over his arms and chest, "that you convinced me to trust you enough to let you try. Jack, you're the only man I've ever known who worked so damned hard to keep me from running. As much as I dreamed about having this—this house, you, my babies, I wasn't willing to put the effort into having them. You made me want to try."

"It took you a while. You ran. More than once, if I remember correctly."

"I was wrong. I'm sorry."

Jack's head fell back as he gave out a jubilant laugh.

"You're laughing at me?"

"Molly, this is the first time you've ever admitted to being wrong. I never thought I'd hear you say the words."

She made the cutest pout with a mouth that had driven him wild in countless dreams. "I can take the words back if you think they're so funny."

"No, don't do that. Please. I'm sorry for laughing, honest." Jack got to his feet and pulled Molly up with him. "I accept your apology."

"I love you."

He kissed her. It was a soft kiss, one filled with tenderness and understanding. Molly hugged his neck and held him as close to her as her large belly would allow and moaned her approval.

"I've still got my pants on," Jack reminded her. "Do you want me to take them off?"

"Rain check?"

"Rain check?" Jack asked, unable to hide his disappointment.

"I've got a massive craving for ice cream. Will you take Arnold and me to the ice cream parlour?"

"Rocky road?"

"No, there's a new flavour I want to try. It's pistachio with chili peppers. It's called Dragon's Breath."

twenty-eight

"We should get married."

"Why?"

"Molly, you're having our children. We live in this beautiful home. We have a dog. We should be married."

"Not a good enough reason, Jack."

Molly put the last spoonful of vanilla ice cream in her mouth and savoured it. She had to give up Dragon's Breath when the heartburn it caused became unbearable.

"I thought that was part of your plan."

"Someday, but not now. I'm not expecting you to ask me, Jack. We're still getting to know each other. There's no rush."

"Having kids isn't an incentive to speed up the process?"

"No, it's not."

"How about love?"

"No. Not love either."

"What would it take for us to get married then?"

"When the time is right, Jack. We'll know when the time is right."

XO XO XO

Molly stretched in their bed, trying not to feel guilty having Jack wait on her around the clock. She couldn't go against doctor's orders, and Jack was more than happy to be at her service. He had only one request.

She had to have a name for both of the twins whenever he did something for her.

She was happy, happier than she ever believed possible. Her nightmares were long gone, and the ghosts that once haunted her had vanished, only to be replaced by a friendly green dragon. She ran her hands over her large belly. The twins were due anytime.

Molly looked forward to meeting her children. They came to her in her dreams, joining Finley for fun and games. They laughed and played and sang silly songs. She knew that Jack was having the same dreams. Sometimes when the twins' kicking kept her awake during the night, she would hear him sing in his sleep. She couldn't make out the words, but the tune was always the same familiar song that filled her dreams.

Jack entered their bedroom dressed only in faded jeans that hung sinfully low on his hips. He'd kept his hair long for her, knowing how much she loved to run her fingers through the long strands when they made love or during pillow talk when they discussed babies' names.

"I still think that Prince and Princess will solve the problem," he said as he handed her a bowl of vanilla ice cream.

"No."

"How about Molly Junior and Jack Junior?"

"No. I told you that before."

"Do you have any names in mind? Like you were supposed to?"

"No."

"Okay, it's time for Plan B. We're going to write out the names we like and decide on the ones we want."

"Makes sense to me, even though we've tried that and failed."

"Not this time," Jack said, grinning mischievously.

She watched him as he pulled out a package of washable magic markers from his back pocket. "What are you doing?"

"We're going to write out our choices for names on your belly. Once your belly is covered, we have to make a decision."

"What if neither of us likes any of the names?"

"Plan C. You have a back, arms and legs, and a mighty fine ass."

"You have legs and an ass, too."

"Ladies first."

"Are you sure this will work?"

"Trust me. I guarantee it."

XO XO XO

"I can't believe you talked me into this," Molly said, her face flushed with embarrassment as he helped her out of her clothes in the hospital delivery room.

"The markers will wash off, I think."

"You think? I'm giving birth to our babies any minute now, and I have all of these stupid names written all over my body!"

"I've got them on my ass, remember."

"No one's going to be looking at your ass, Jack. I'm the one who is naked here."

"I can strip if it would make you happy." He started to unbutton his shirt.

"I hate you."

"But you love me more." Jack reached for her hand and squeezed it. "It will work out. Trust me."

"You know, I'm getting pretty tired of you telling me to trust you. You're not the one who has to push out a couple of bowling balls."

Jack helped her into her hospital gown. "You know I'd do it, sweetheart, but I'd fail miserably."

"Next time, you try it."

"No promises."

Jack helped Molly onto the birthing bed with great care.

"I'm scared, Jack."

"Me, too, but in a good way."

"You'll be an awesome father. Think of the stories you can tell our children. You'll be the only living and breathing storybook on two legs."

"Very funny."

"I'm serious."

"You'll be a spectacular mother."

"You think so?"

"I know so."

"We have to pick names, Jack."

"Let's wait until they're born. Lots of parents don't name their children until a few days, even weeks after they arrive. They like to get a feel for the child's personality before they burden them with a name."

"You were the one who started this. We're picking names now."

"Fine."

Jack pulled up Molly's gown past her belly.

"Hey!"

"Relax. You don't have anything the nurses haven't seen before. Let's go through these names once more just to be sure."

"Jack, none of those names are good enough."

He read the names aloud quickly, "Bobby, Billy, William, Waldo, Matthew, Bronson, Patrick."

"No."

"Belinda, Emily, Frances, Hillary, Harriet, Molly Junior."

"No. I told you none of those names work."

"Okay. Here is what we're going to do." Jack pulled out a marker from his back pocket and wrote two names on his left arm. When he finished, he drew the outline of a rose around each one.

"What did you write?"

"The names of our children."

"Jack, what did you write?"

"Molly, do you trust me? Yes, or no?"

She looked deep into his twinkling blue eyes and saw his love for her. How could she not trust him? "Yes, I trust you."

"Good. It's decided." Jack showed Molly his arm.

"You didn't!"

"I did."

"I hate you, dragon slayer."

"But you love me, and you love them, too."

twenty-nine

Molly loved standing on the sidelines watching Dragon Slayers perform in concert. She appreciated all the labor and teamwork it took to put on a concert, often teasing Jack that writing the songs was the easy part. All of the crew adored her and made sure she had the best vantage point for watching her husband perform. It also kept her in Jack's line of sight, allowing him to send her a nod or blow her a kiss whenever he wanted.

Tonight was different. It was Jack's thirtieth birthday, and Molly had planned a big surprise for him. Axl, Ben and Matt were in on the surprise and made sure that everything was in place to make it work.

"It's almost time," one of the stage crew announced to Molly. "Once they finish this song, you can head out. He'll be switching guitars on the other side of the stage, so he won't see you coming."

Molly nodded her head. She could feel her heart racing. She'd never been on stage with Jack before, especially in front of thousands of his fans. She hoped she wouldn't screw this up. She glanced to her side and saw the trolley with the chocolate fudge birthday cake. Two crew members were busy lighting the thirty candles.

Molly looked down at Jack's birthday surprise. The twins stood still as another crewmember made sure their ear protectors were positioned correctly on their heads. They looked adorable in their new Dragon Slayers T-Shirts and faded jeans. Just like Daddy.

"How's that?" she heard him ask them.

They answered with a thumbs up.

"Go!"

"Give me your hands, please."

The twins took hold of her hands, and they walked on stage. Even with earplugs, Molly found the noise overwhelming. She wondered what the twins thought of the noise. She could see Axl smiling at them as they approached.

"Are you ready?" he asked them.

"Yes!" the twins yelled at him.

"Go to Daddy."

Molly let go of their hands, and the twins ran toward Jack. Immediately the audience cheered the twins on. When Jack saw what all the cheering was about, he dropped to his knees and held out his arms to catch them.

"Happy birthday, Daddy," they yelled. The twins were hooked up to microphones so that when Axl started to play *Happy Birthday*, they would be heard singing to their father. "Happy birthday to you . . ."

Molly could see the sparkle in Jack's eyes and his tears. She took hold of the trolley's handle and pushed it toward Jack and the twins. She had reached them by the time they finished singing.

The audience cheered and applauded when Jack got to his feet holding a twin in each arm. They leaned over the cake and blew out the candles. Jack motioned for Molly to join him. She kissed him long enough to let the audience know that he belonged to her.

The audience became quiet to let Jack speak. "In case you didn't know, it's my thirtieth birthday today."

Cheers filled the air.

"This is the best birthday present I've ever had. Thanks to my beautiful wife, Molly, and our children, Finley and Fiona. And in case you can't tell, we're having another one in a couple of months."

"What's this one's name going to be?" Axl shouted out.

Jack gazed at Molly, his eyes filled with a love that let her know she could always trust him.

"Tell me," she said, smiling. "Anything but Goliath. That's just too weird."

"Angus," Jack replied. "After your dad. This time we'll have a name from your story."

Molly reached for Jack and kissed him. "I love you," she said softly.

"I know," Jack answered. "Forever."

recipe .... O

book club .... O

about the author .... O

Davina + Quinn series .... O

other books by
Deborah Armstrong .... O

stay connected........................... O

Jack and Stevie's Favourite Chocolate Chip Cookies

Maggie always makes sure to bake a batch of these cookies when she's visiting her favourite twins. Maggie adds an extra ½ cup of chocolate to make the cookies extra chocolatey.

Prep time about 15 minutes

Baking time under 30 minutes

Ingredients:

2½ cups all-purpose flour

2 cups packed light brown sugar

2 large eggs

½ teaspoon sea salt

8 tablespoons (1 stick) unsalted butter at room temperature

1 ½ teaspoons pure vanilla extract

1 ½ cups semisweet chocolate chips (or more)

1 heaping teaspoon baking soda

Preheat oven to 350 F. Position rack in the centre of the oven. Line a baking sheet with parchment paper.

In a medium bowl, whisk together the flour, baking soda, and salt. Set aside.

In a large bowl, beat the butter and sugar on medium-high speed until light and fluffy (2-3 minutes). Add the eggs and beat until blended. Add the vanilla and beat until blended.

Turn the mixer off and add the flour mixture to the bowl. Mix on medium just until the flour is mixed in, then turn the mixer to high speed for a few seconds to pull the dough together. It will be chunky.

Add the chocolate chips and beat on high for about 5 seconds to thoroughly mix in the chips.

Drop by large spoonfuls on the lined baking sheet. Don't flatten them. Bake until lightly browned on top – about 10 to 11 minutes.

Cool on the pan for 1 minute, then transfer the cookies to a rack to cool completely. Repeat with the remaining dough.

Makes about 40 cookies.

book club questions

1. How did the book make you feel?
   - Were you intrigued by Jack and Molly's story?
   - Are you glad you read it?

2. What did you think about the main characters?
   - Were they believable?
   - Which character did you relate to the most/least?
   - Was Jack's virginity something you admire?
   - Was Molly's hot headedness too much?
   - If you were to be one of the characters, who would you be? Why?

3. Which parts of the book stood out to you?
   - Are there quotes, passages, or scenes that you found particularly compelling?
   - Were there scenes that you found to be unique, thought-provoking, or disturbing?

4. What themes did you detect in the story?
   - Have you ever been in a situation where something terrified you?
   - Have you ever been asked to trust someone without question?
   - Have you ever had to overlook or accept something so that you could have a relationship with someone?

5. What did you think about the ending?

- Were you satisfied or disappointed with how it ended?

- How do you picture the characters' lives after the end of the story?

6. What changes/decisions would you hope for if the story were made into a movie?

- Is there anything you would cut from the book?

- Who would you cast to play the main characters?

7. How does this book compare to other romance novels you've read?

- Do you want to read more in the series?

8. What is your impression of the author?

- What do you think of the author's writing style?

- What do you think of the author's story telling ability?

- Would you read another book by the same author?

about the author

Deborah Armstrong hit the big 50, and became restless and couldn't concentrate on much. Her favourite escape was to read. Instantly, her daughter's romance novels became the ultimate magnet. Hours were spent devouring them.

That was then ... this is now. Deborah turned her restlessness into writing hot and spicy contemporary romance with a touch of country.

Deborah lives with her husband and five hundred cows on their dairy farm in Ontario, Canada. When she's not writing or working on the farm, she enjoys reading, travelling, watching movies, and spending time with friends and family, especially her grandchildren. She also proofreads and edits for fellow authors. Her writing muse tends to run on the liquid side: strong coffee, chocolate milk, and single malt scotch in no particular order.

Thrice each week, the local gym beckons. Cardio means book thinking time for unravelling plots and conversations for her current work in progress.

When Deborah's characters talk, she listens. Not surprisingly, they decide when and how to tell their story, talking to her at the strangest times. When she's driving, working out, or trying to fall asleep, they whisper in her ear and say, "this is what needs to happen next."

Other books in the series

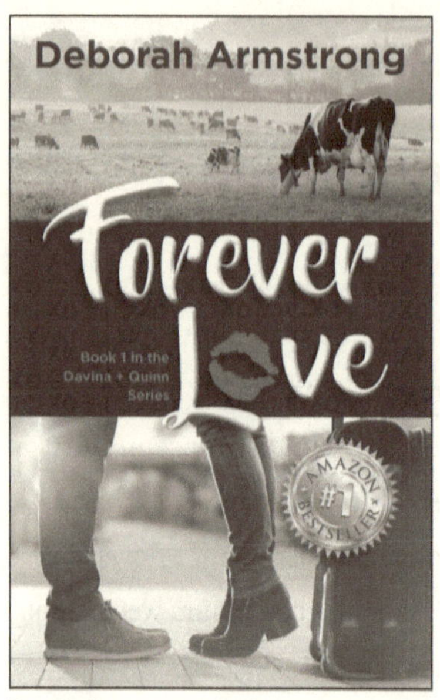

Book 1

Book 2

Book 3

Novella

Also by Deborah Armstrong

stay connected

Deborah Armstrong is a storyteller, creating fantasies and weaving them for your reading delight from her farm in Ontario, Canada.

If you are in a Book Club, bring Deborah to yours via Skype, Zoom . . .or in person! Whether it's a hot and steamy summer day or one kissed with a wintry landscape, have your Club gather their favourite snacks and beverages and discover the Davina and Quinn series. Deborah invites her readers to follow her on social media and to contact her by email. To work with her, visit her website and subscribe to her newsletter.

Website: DeborahArmstrong.ca

 WriterDeborah

 deboraharmstrongauthor/

 DeborahArmstrongAuthor

 deborah_armstrong_author/

 author/show/6467157.Deborah_Armstrong